THERE'S J

Antonio Castillo

6'+, long and lean
brown eyes, brown hair
flirtatious and fun-loving
with a sexy smile and adorable dimples—
a natural with kids
royalty
and a full-blooded Latin lover!

**It's American Romance with more passion,
more intensity…
and more male sex appeal!**

Dear Reader,

Welcome to another month of wonderful stories at Harlequin American Romance—where you'll find more of what you love to read. Every month we'll bring you a variety of plots from some of the genre's best-loved authors. Harlequin American Romance is all about the pursuit of love and family in the backyards, big cities and wide-open spaces of America!

This month you won't want to miss *A Cowboy's Woman*, the continuation of Cathy Gillen Thacker's series, THE McCABES OF TEXAS. This family of bachelors is in for some surprises when their parents take to matchmaking. And talented author Muriel Jensen brings us *Countdown to Baby*, the second book in the DELIVERY ROOM DADS series. In this three-author, three-book series you'll meet the McIntyre brothers of Bison City, Wyoming. They're in a race to see who'll have the New Year's first baby.

Also this month is Mollie Molay's *Daddy by Christmas*, a compelling story of blended families— just in time for the holidays. And Mindy Neff wraps up her TALL, DARK & IRRESISTIBLE duo with *The Playboy & the Mommy*.

Please drop us a note to tell us what you love about Harlequin American Romance and what you'd like to see in the future. Write to us c/o Harlequin Books, 300 East 42nd Street, 6th Floor, New York, NY 10017.

Happy reading!

Melissa Jeglinski
Associate Senior Editor

The Playboy & the Mommy

MINDY NEFF

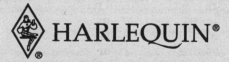

HARLEQUIN®

TORONTO • NEW YORK • LONDON
AMSTERDAM • PARIS • SYDNEY • HAMBURG
STOCKHOLM • ATHENS • TOKYO • MILAN • MADRID
PRAGUE • WARSAW • BUDAPEST • AUCKLAND

For Roland and David:

True heroes, wonderful friends and the
best two brothers a girl could ask for.
Thanks for always being there, guys.

ISBN 0-373-16800-4

THE PLAYBOY & THE MOMMY

Copyright © 1999 by Melinda Neff.

Visit us at www.romance.net

Printed in U.S.A.

ABOUT THE AUTHOR

Originally from Louisiana, Mindy Neff settled in Southern California where she married a really romantic guy and raised five great kids. Family, friends, writing and reading are her passions. When not writing, Mindy's ideal getaway is a good book, hot sunshine and a chair at the river's edge with water lapping at her toes.

Mindy loves to hear from readers and can be reached at P.O. Box 2704-262, Huntington Beach, CA 92647.

Books by Mindy Neff

HARLEQUIN AMERICAN ROMANCE

Dear Reader,

When I wrote the launch book for the Harlequin American Romance miniseries, THE ULTIMATE..., I realized that not only were these men "every woman's fantasy, but only one woman's dream come true," there was just something about the way a Latin man looks at a woman, the way he touches her, that lets her *know* she's a woman.

Antonio Castillo, hero of *The Playboy & the Mommy*, was one such man for me. This commitment-shy playboy can be the consummate lover, or friend, whichever a woman chooses. But when he meets Chelsa Lawrence and her two little girls, this playboy suddenly has marriage and family in mind.

I hope you'll enjoy the final book in my TALL, DARK & IRRESISTIBLE duo, and that you'll have as much fun revisiting the Latin lovers from HAR #711 *They're the One!* (1/98) and HAR #795 *The Virgin & Her Bodyguard* (10/99) as I had writing about them!

I love to hear from readers. Please write to me at P.O. Box 2704-262, Huntington Beach, CA 92647.

Warmest Regards,

Mindy Neff

Chapter One

Chelsa Lawrence sat on the enclosed porch of her rented bungalow, her arms wrapped around her two daughters. A storm had slammed into the Mediterranean coast, fierce and unforgiving, turning the small island of San Alegra into a state of unstable anticipation. The surf pounded and the wind howled. It was almost midnight and Chelsa knew the girls should've been in bed hours ago, but the fear of tidal waves and rooftops blown off by winds had both little girls huddled close, watching the specter of nature unfold.

Their imaginations were vivid, as was their mother's. After all, the children's books Chelsa wrote, *The Adventures of Water Babies,* were fashioned after her own girls, Emily and Sophie. Chelsa marveled at their little minds, their endless questions, and used them in the stories she wrote.

But tonight her thoughts weren't on sweet, innocent stories. Perhaps it was the ferocious intensity of the storm, but she felt a sense of foreboding.

Her arms tightened. She would keep her daughters safe.

"Momma, you're squishing the bref out of me."

"Sorry, Sophie." She eased her grip on her four-year-old.

"Momma?" This time it was Emily's quiet voice. "Do you think that boat will hit the rocks?"

"Hmm?" She hadn't noticed a boat.

Sophie wiggled out of her hold and perched forward on the bench. "Pirates," she whispered.

"There's no such thing as pirates," Emily admonished. Being six, she felt her knowledge was much more superior than her younger sister's.

"Uh-huh! 'Member Hook? And Tinker Bell?"

"That's just movies, silly. Right, Momma?" Superior, she might be, but still a little girl who got scared.

"Yes, sweetie. It's just a movie. But it's fun to imagine." Of course, there were still pirates roaming the seas, but none so dramatic as the movies might depict.

"See!" Sophie chirped and rested pudgy hands on equally pudgy knees. Emily rolled her eyes because her little sister still didn't get it.

Chelsa stood. Pirate or not, that boat was in grave danger. The sea roiled and spat, tossing the sleek craft around like a rubber duck in a washing machine. Waves crashed over the rocks that jutted maybe fifty yards off shore, cascading over the sides in a beard of frothy foam. It appeared the skipper was attempting to head for the beach, but the gusty winds and churning swells thwarted his efforts.

Her heart started to pound and adrenaline kicked in. The beach was pitch-black, illuminated only by the light of a partial moon against the foamy crest of the waves. The power was out in the house and the phone lines were down. If the ship crashed, there would be no way to call for help.

But then, Chelsa shouldn't even be considering calling for help. She had no business getting involved, especially since there was no telling who was aboard that ship—including a modern-day pirate.

And at all costs, she had her children to think about. Their safety.

In a matter of two weeks or less, their lives could very well be in danger. All of their lives.

A sinister blast of wind sprayed sand and sea salt, testing the strength of the screen door. The pounding of angry water against unforgiving rock superseded the sound of splintering wood as the yacht lost its control against nature and slammed into the rocks. Like straw in a dust devil, debris scattered, whirling, projected into the air, flung high and wide at the mercy of the storm.

And in that instant before impact, Chelsa saw someone dive for safety. The girls were jumping now, both terrified and excited.

"Momma! The rocks breaked the boat!" Sophie screamed.

"Momma! A man jumped over the side!"

"Yes," Chelsa said, her hand hesitating at the screen door, indecision screaming within her.

"Go get him, Momma."

"Wait," she said. "Hush, now." She had to think, didn't quite know what to do.

"But he's not swimming. He's just floating," Emily said.

"You gotta get him, Momma," Sophie said, her solemn blue eyes round with worry. "Willy can't save him in the big waves."

She was talking about the whale in *Free Willy*. Her children watched entirely too many movies, Chelsa decided.

And they expected her to be a heroine. She'd never felt less like a heroine in her life. But with two sets of expectant, round eyes looking up at her, she had little choice.

"Stay right here. Both of you. Don't move a muscle. Do you understand?" At their twin nods, Chelsa kicked off her sandals and raced across the cool sand.

She saw him surface. Like a bodysurfer with the aid of unseen hands, he rode the crest of a wave, the momentum dumping him onshore right at her feet. Battling winds that slashed at her clothes, whipping her hair in a wild frenzy, she flipped him over, gripped him beneath his arms and tugged. Wet and shaking, adrenaline lent her strength as she dragged him free of the fierce current.

The horrendous weather was like an omen, an evil one. She felt exposed, yet knew she was overreacting. Her life was in chaos, though, and the weight of it was sucking her down, much like the ocean was swallowing the remains of the boat.

She set those thoughts aside for the moment and checked her beached sailor. He was breathing, thank goodness, but his eyes were closed.

"Can you hear me?" she shouted over the force of the storm.

He didn't respond. Unconscious. And no wonder. With the way that yacht had exploded against the rocks, it was a miracle he was even drawing a breath.

"Is he dead?"

"Is there any blood?"

Her head whipped around. "I thought I told you girls to stay on the porch!"

"Sophie got scared," Emily blamed.

"Nuh-uh!"

"Stop it, both of you. I don't need this right now."

The girls flanked her, wrapping their arms around her in apology.

Chelsa took a steadying breath. "Sorry, girls. Momma didn't mean to shout."

"That's okay," Emily said. "What are you going to do with the man?"

"Get him to the house, I guess." And get her daughters out of the open, exposed, where anyone might see or harm them. Fear over being seen doubled her determination. Stretched out on the wet sand, the man appeared to be over six feet. And he outweighed her by a good eighty pounds.

But there was no one else to rely on for help, a truth she'd become all too familiar with lately.

With the hem of her dress swirling around her ankles, threatening to trip her, she waded into the tide and snagged a piece of canvas before the surf could carry it out again. She didn't know a lot about fancy yachts, but it was obvious this was part of the sail. Once again, she realized this man should be counting his blessings. It would take horrendous force to rip this sturdy canvas. It was a wonder this man's body wasn't in the same shape.

Praying she wasn't setting herself up for a lawsuit over moving an individual who might have a neck injury, she rolled him onto the canvas and tugged.

His feet cut deep furrows in the sand as she back-tracked the hundred or so yards to the bungalow. Straining, her shoulder muscles feeling like they were on fire, she managed to drag him into the house—though the porch steps scraping along his back gave her grief and made her wince. The girls were more hindrance than help, but she didn't have the heart to tell them so. They were so proud of themselves for doing their part.

For an instant, she considered making him comfortable outside, in the screened-in porch, but that offended her ingrained Southern hospitality. Her own mother would've had a fit.

By the time she had him settled in the bed, she was exhausted. Candles burned, casting a shadowy glow over his still features.

When she got a good look, she sucked in a breath.

Oh, no. Handsome as sin. Easily recognizable.

Her heart raced as she charged to the window and jerked down the shade.

"Emily, lock the doors. Sophie, go with your sister."

"Why—"

"Just do as I say. And stay inside."

The last thing she needed was the possibility of lurking photographers, some hungry journalist snapping pictures of her girls. And where this man went, paparazzi were sure to follow.

She took another breath and looked back at the unconscious, soaked man lying in her bed. Hands trembling, she fisted them and ordered herself to relax.

There was work to be done still—the highly interesting task of undressing this virile, exquisitely thrilling celebrity.

The royal Don Juan who set both Latin and American women's hearts aflutter.

Even in repose, he oozed charm. And the instant she touched his bare skin, she learned that a harried mother of two from Mississippi wasn't in any way immune to the magnetic draw of Prince Antonio Castillo of Valldoria.

SOMEONE WAS POUNDING on his head. He pried his eyes open and was immediately sorry that he'd done so. The throbbing increased.

But the vision wasn't too bad. *An angel,* he thought.

Before he could fully appreciate the magnificent sight, two cherubs bounced on the bed. Well, only one of them bounced. The other stood next to the bed, right by his head, poking at the dimple in his cheek that stayed indented whether he was smiling or not.

And he was not at the moment. The pain hammering away at his temples was excruciating.

Three females hovered over him—two miniature and one nicely put together. *Very* nicely put together.

He felt at a distinct disadvantage. Even under the incessant throb of his head, he had enough sense to realize he was naked beneath the wedding ring quilt. And he didn't imagine he'd been the one to do the undressing.

"Good morning, Your Highness," the lovely vision said.

Ah, Antonio thought. *Southern.* He was a man who had a weakness for women with those sexy American drawls.

Then he realized what she'd called him, and he laughed. A big mistake. Nausea churned at the sharp pain, but he dismissed it. He'd crashed million-dollar race cars and been in worse shape. A knock on the head from a damaged sailboat was of little concern.

"Good morning to you, too. And Antonio will do fine. My brother, Joseph is the heir, I'm just the spare. Where am I?"

"On your island."

"Valldoria's not an island."

"No, San Alegra."

"Ah. The land of happiness. At least familiar ground."

Chelsa put a trembling hand on Sophie's shoulder before the child could poke Antonio Castillo's dimples again. That smooth-as-silk Latin accent sent shivers up and down her spine. The man might denounce his title, but he was still a prince by right of birth. A reputed *playboy* prince.

Even with the goose-egg-size bump on his golden-brown forehead that was fast turning an interesting shade of purple, he was handsome as sin. The myriad photographs taken of him around the globe didn't do him a bit of justice.

Good night, if she wasn't careful, she'd be the one stroking those dimples rather than her daughter.

"Did you buy the whole ocean?" Emily asked.

"No, little *diosa*. Just the land. And technically it is my family who owns it."

She giggled. "What's dossa?"

"*Diosa*," Antonio pronounced, tickled by the little girl's infectious laughter. He appreciated laughter in any form. "Goddess."

The little cherub next to the bed crept closer. "Like da lil' mermaid?"

"Something like."

"Girls, go have your breakfast and leave Mr., uh…"

"Tony," he supplied, realizing she was hesitating for fear of creating a faux pas over calling a prince by his surname. But Antonio wasn't one to stand on ceremony. Any ceremony. "And you are?"

"Chelsa. These are my daughters, Emily and Sophie. Go now, girls."

"But Momma," they chorused.

"No buts." Her voice was soft, with a firmness that commanded instant attention and action. "Sophie, you let Emily pour the milk this time."

Antonio noticed that the littlest one started to object then apparently thought better of it. Ignoring the evil ghoul in his head wielding a hammer, he got a tighter grip on the quilt when Emily bounced down off the mattress. His lips kicked up in admiration as he watched the girls scramble to obey their mother.

And oh, what a mother, he thought, always one to appreciate loveliness. She wasn't beautiful like the starlets he normally gravitated toward. "Wholesome" was how he'd describe this woman. Blond hair, streaked by nothing stronger than the sunlight, created a curly, shoulder-length halo around a smooth, peaches-and-cream complexion. He imagined the humidity would play the very devil with all that natural curl. A sprinkling of freckles kissed the bridge of her nose. Clear blue eyes, unadorned by cosmetics, were round and intelligent…and just a bit wary.

To Antonio's way of thinking, it was a sin for any woman to display wariness in his presence, and he set about to correct it.

"Tell me, *bella,* is it just Chelsa, or do you have a last name?"

She took a step back and folded her hands at her waist. Short nails, he noted, no artificial tips or polish. And no wedding ring.

The wariness he'd detected flickered in her eyes like sparklers on Independence day. His curiosity and hero's heart went on full alert. He loved women of all shapes and sizes, their smell, their softness, their quirks. It was both a talent and an obsession to learn what made them tick.

But patience was a virtue and Antonio had plenty of it. Any man with a set of eyes could see that beneath the exterior of reserve were banked passions and fire. He wanted to know what made her hide behind all that Southern poise.

At last she unknotted her hands and tugged at a wrinkle on the quilt. "It's Lawrence. Chelsa Lawrence."

He reached out and took her hand in his. "I am pleased to meet you, Chelsa Lawrence. And I believe I may well owe you my life." Slowly he brought her fingertips to his lips and kissed the back of her knuckles, his gaze holding hers. "Thank you, *bella.*"

Chelsa wasn't sure she could draw a breath, much less speak, but she gave it a shot. "You're…" She cleared her throat and straightened, easing her hand away. Good night, she hadn't felt a zing like that in a long time…if ever. "You're welcome. And speaking of saving, I looked as best I could with the storm and all, but I didn't see evidence of anyone else with you when the yacht hit the reef."

"No. I was captain and crew alone."

She shouldn't have been astonished, but she was. "On a ship that size? Not very sensible."

"Ah, but I am excellent at what I do. *All* that I do."

She saw the flirtatious challenge in his dark eyes and wickedly sensual smile. She might have been put off by bragging, but his widely publicized reputation substantiated the claim.

Latin Lover. At last she understood the meaning, or at least the draw. With a mere look, a simple touch, he made her feel utterly, exquisitely female. And with a probable concussion at that. *Talk about potent,* she thought, barely resisting the urge to fan herself.

But she hadn't traveled—or run, rather—across an entire continent to swoon beneath the power of a man's confidence and sex appeal.

"Perhaps not *all* that you do. Otherwise your fancy boat wouldn't look like a pile of toothpicks littering the beach." She saw his dimples deepen, saw the corners of his lips start to climb and knew she had to get out of here. "I imagine you're probably hungry, so I'll go fix you some breakfast. It'll only be cold cereal. The power's still out from the storm."

Her hormones screaming like a Mississippi steam engine, she fled the room, the sound of his soft laughter following in her wake.

Dear heaven, he was the wrong man to elicit such a powerful response. A reputed playboy, Prince Antonio Castillo of Valldoria was both recognizable and newsworthy worldwide, not only in the tabloids and gossip columns, but in the sports pages of every major newspaper across the country.

And whoever happened to be with him garnered national headlines, as well.

Rick was an avid sports fan. He'd never had much interest in the tabloids, but newspapers were a different matter—an obsession actually for a man who tossed his ante in every bet pool available.

And she had a fairly good idea he'd have access to the sports pages in that cushy Mississippi penitentiary.

She couldn't take a chance on him finding out her whereabouts. If he did, she might as well kiss her life—and the lives of her daughters—goodbye.

NOT ONE TO LAY about in bed, Antonio wrapped the sheet around himself and gingerly sat up on the side of the mattress. So far so good. A little woozy, a sharp edge of pain, but manageable.

From the bay window facing the ocean, he watched a moody moment of changing light and drama. The bluster and blow of the coastal squall had passed, and for now the sea was calm and the winds quiet. To the east, a tranquil window of fleeting sunlight vied for position with the persistent after-grays, neither ready to concede the slowly clearing sky.

Sure enough, debris of the *Diablo Plata* was strewn on the pristine sand. He was sorry about the loss. It was a sweet sloop; he'd won two first-place cups in the sleek beauty.

From the looks of the pitiful remains, though, he was lucky to be alive.

The sound of little-girl giggles and the soft, Southern drawl of his hostess drew his attention. A cursory search of the room didn't turn up his clothes, so he settled for a flowery kimono he found hanging from a hook on the back of the bathroom door. Chelsa's obviously. It carried a hint of her scent. Citrus. The shoulder seams strained a bit, but he managed to get the robe tied at the middle to preserve his modesty.

Not that he was all that modest, but there were *niñas* in the house.

He nearly collided with Chelsa in the doorway of the kitchen. As it was, the bed tray smacked him in the stomach—a stomach, he realized, that was tender. Obviously he hadn't taken a complete inventory of his injuries other than the throbbing in his head.

He placed his hands over hers, steadying the tray. Milk sloshed over the rim of the cereal bowl.

"Careful," he said, noticing that her hands trembled. *Excitement?* he wondered. *Or fear.* There was something about this woman that made him think of a damsel in distress.

"You shouldn't be out of bed."

She wore a tank-style dress that hung from spaghetti straps and skimmed her body right down to her bare toes. He wanted to spend a good long while just staring at her, drinking in the soft cadence of her sexy Southern drawl.

But they had an avid audience and Antonio was a man who valued privacy when it came to intimacies and wooing. "A little bump on the head won't keep me down."

"Lord save me from macho men. Suit yourself." She let go of the tray and stepped away. Good thing he had a decent hold on the plastic or there'd have been a mess.

Antonio grinned and set the tray on the table where the two little girls were spelling words with their alphabet cereal. "We meet again, *mi bellas*. May I join you?"

Emily giggled. Sophie, her pudgy cheeks full, simply looked up at him with round, innocent eyes.

"You're wearing Momma's robe," Emily said.

"Ah, little goddess, you are astute to be noticing fashion at such a young age. Do you not consider it quite the thing?" He held his arms out to his sides like a European model on a runway, careful not to rip the satin.

Emily went off in another gale of laughter. Sophie, the solemn little cherub, popped the spoon out of her mouth. "Boys aren't s'posed to wear flowers."

"Sophie!" Chelsa scolded. Antonio noticed that she was making a valiant attempt to keep a lid on her amusement. Her enticing lips quivered charmingly at the corners.

It didn't bother him a bit that the amusement was at his expense. "That is quite all right, little mermaid." Sophie's eyes widened in thought at the title. "Boys might object to the silliness of flowers, but when they grow up to be men, they soon learn that if they feel strong on the inside, the outside package doesn't matter."

Emily bobbed her head. "Cuz they're secure in their mask'a'linty."

He felt his brows shoot upward. "How old are you, goddess?"

"Six," Emily said, straightening importantly in her chair.

"Ah, yes. That would explain why you know about such things as masculinity." He spared a glance at Chelsa, who appeared resigned rather than scandalized by her daughter's announcement.

"'Course she knows 'bout it," Sophie inserted. "Cuz of the water babies."

"The water babies?" Perhaps the bump on his head was more severe than he had first determined.

He was suddenly and thoroughly lost in the conversation.

"Yep," Sophie said, as if that were that.

He looked at Chelsa for clarification. She appeared to be waging a battle with herself over divulging information, as though she were guarding an international secret. Before she could come to a decision, though, Emily picked up the thread of explanation.

"Momma writes *The Adventures of Water Babies.*"

"*The Adventures of Water Babies?*" *Dios,* he was becoming a parrot.

"Children's books, silly."

His brows shot up again. He liked kids well enough—other people's kids, that was—and these two little imps intrigued the hell out of him.

He grinned. "Yes, silly me. Of course they're for children. That would be why I have never read them."

"You could if you wanted. Momma gots lots of copies."

"Girls," Chelsa said. "I'm sure Mr. Castillo isn't interested in—"

"Tony," he corrected. "And I *am* interested. However, we have become sidetracked from the original subject of flowers and feminine wear and masculinity. And Emily was about to be so charming as to enlighten me."

"Well," Emily drawled, pleased to hold center stage, "when the water baby frog was messin' around and fell off the lily pad, the wicked old cricket laughed at him and made fun. And the water baby should'a got all embarrassed cuz the ladybug with the flirty eyelashes was watchin' him. But he climbed right back on the lily pad—even though his face was red and he was now wearing a daisy on his head like a lady's church hat—and he winked at the ladybug and smiled real big like, just as pretty as you please. That's cuz he was secure in his mask'a'linty—''

''Masculinity,'' Antonio coached.

Emily nodded. ''And the ladybug thought that was very special. The water baby didn't get mad and he went right on wearing the flower like it was meant to be, and it was the cricket who felt like the silly one for acting so ugly and pokin' fun.'' She folded her hands primly in front of her on the table, suddenly looking much older than her years. ''But I'm sure my little sister wasn't makin' fun of you in Momma's robe.''

Sophie shook her head from side to side, sending her cap of frizzy blond curls swinging. She'd been as caught up in the tale as though she'd never heard it before. ''Nuh-uh.''

Something warm and gentle passed though Antonio as he studied these three beautiful acquaintances he'd literally dropped in on. He liked the soft smile that transformed Chelsa Lawrence's smooth features as she'd listened to her daughter regale him with stories. A story she'd evidently written. And he was more than a little in love with these heartbreaker cherubs who said whatever crossed their young minds.

''Of course you were not making fun,'' he said to Sophie. ''I am sure you both have excellent manners. Actually, it is I who should apologize to such fine ladies for appearing in the dining hall wearing night-clothes.'' The tiny breakfast area was hardly formal, but he got a kick out of surprising reactions out of the children. "However, I could not find evidence of my own garments… I do hope I arrived with them?"

Both little girls giggled. "Momma taked 'em off you."

Their mother flushed scarlet.

He met her eyes, thinking it was a crying shame he hadn't been awake and alert for the undressing. A first for him. When a beautiful woman stripped him naked, he liked to be a participant.

"They're in the dryer," Chelsa said.

"Still wet, I would imagine, since we as yet have no power."

"Yes. I rinsed them by hand."

"You should not have gone to the trouble. I could have done that myself."

Her blond brows lifted, though her cheeks still glowed like the blush of a new peach. "A prince does laundry?"

"This lowly one does. I travel alone a lot. At sea, I do not carry the staff with me."

"You should at least employ a crew."

"At times I do. However, had I been sailing with a full crew, your bungalow would be bursting at the seams and I doubt you would possess enough garments to clothe them all."

If he hadn't been watching closely, he would have missed the slight tightening at the corners of her clear blue eyes. Obviously this woman wasn't keen on having her privacy invaded. He wondered why. Those questions would best be asked in private, he decided. Whatever caused her to grow silent and wary, however fleeting, was probably something she would rather shield her little girls from.

Then again, he could be all wrong. Perhaps she was simply annoyed at having her vacation interrupted.

With his brain finally revving up to speed, another thought struck him like a lightning bolt straight from the gods. A question any respectable playboy was reluctant to voice, but Antonio knew he must. He glanced once more at her unadorned finger, then back to her clear, lake-blue eyes.

"I have apparently lost the last twelve hours or so of my memory, and it has rattled my decent manners. Perhaps it will appear unseemly and in poor taste if your husband were to return while I sit in your breakfast nook wearing your robe...?" He let the words trail off, but his sheepish smile soon faded.

The sudden silence in the small bungalow was strained and thick enough to cut with a machete. Outside, the surf rolled onshore and ebbed out. A gull wheeled overhead with a high-pitched cry, and its mate answered.

As though it were a prearranged, choreographed movement, Chelsa stepped behind her daughters and put a protective hand on each of their shoulders. Emily reached beneath the table and took her sister's hand.

"I'm no longer married."

"Oh." He wasn't sure what to say, or how to say it. Had the man died? The protective circle the three Lawrence females presented told him something wasn't right.

He wasn't in any way prepared for four-year-old Sophie's matter-of-fact declaration.

"My daddy got put in the jailhouse."

Chapter Two

Out of the mouths of babes.

As though shocked into compliance, the power chose that exact moment to come on. The refrigerator hummed and lights flickered over the kitchen sink, competing pitifully with the morning sun.

Antonio wasn't certain how to respond to little Sophie's news. He lived by the motto Live And Let Live, and didn't in any way hold the shady deeds of Chelsa's ex against her—whatever they may be—but he was indeed curious.

However, Chelsa's face had lost a good deal of its color, and the two little imps sitting as still as china dolls were way too solemn.

His gaze met Chelsa's for just an instant. In her eyes he saw both shame and shoulder squaring strength. He'd speak with her alone. Later. In the meantime, a subject change was in order.

"Well, we now have lights on all of the subjects." He flicked a finger down little Sophie's nose. "And with the press of a button, the dryer will have me in decent clothes in no time. And I promise you, *sirena*, not a single flower graces my jeans."

"What's *sirena?*"

"Mermaid." He glanced at Chelsa, noticing her grateful look that he'd managed to sidetrack her daughter.

"I don't gots long hair like Ariel. But Emily does. And Momma," Sophie said with pursed lips and a slight frown.

Ariel was the animated character in the little mermaid movie, he recalled. He looked at Sophie's cap of short, frizzy curls and reached out to touch. Baby soft, silky, yet thick and unruly. A shorter version of her mother's. And though he longed to run his hands through Chelsa's hair, he didn't think she'd stand still for it. So he contented himself with the baby's, allowed his imagination to roam in anticipation of privacy with one Chelsa Lawrence.

Right now, though, he had a tiny girl's ego to attend to. And he was excellent at attending to feminine egos.

"Any mermaid should know when it is time to cut her tresses. You shall be the leader of a trend. And soon, all the mermaids in the sea will realize what a nuisance it is to battle long locks of hair, and they will fashion themselves after you."

"Really?"

"I am certain of it. In fact, sometime I will tell you the story of a very good friend of mine, a beautiful heiress, who boldly left her sacred locks on the floor of a beauty salon in France."

Sophie twined a finger in one of her many curls, her lip poking out. "Was it fuzzy?"

No. It was straight and silky. "Maybe a little. Fuzzy is quite chic."

Sophie perked up.

Emily, anxious to be included, aimed a smirk at

her sibling. "A goddess is more lovely than a mermaid."

"Nuh-uh!"

"Uh-huh."

"Girls," Chelsa warned.

"Beauty is universal," Antonio inserted quickly before things could turn ugly. "We must not say that one shines brighter than the other."

Sophie poked her tongue out at her sister who continued to smirk.

Chelsa rolled her eyes.

Antonio leaned back in his chair and laughed, the exuberance reminding him that ghouls were still having a grand fiesta in his head.

"You should rest," Chelsa said quietly, setting a glass of juice before him along with a couple of pain relievers. He could tell she was still upset that her daughter had aired a piece of their dirty laundry, but she hid it well beneath a steady armor of poise.

Before she could withdraw her hand, he reached for it, drawing her knuckles to his lips. "Thank you, *bella*. You have been very gracious to care for me."

She leaned close, her citrus scent enveloping him like a rich cloud of invigorating tranquility. "Flattery may work on my daughters, but I'm much older and wiser."

"Ah, no, *querida*, a woman is never too old for flattery. Especially when it is genuine."

"Your reputation precedes you, Prince Antonio. You're notorious for passing out compliments. Too much of a good thing tends to get diluted."

"You wound me," he said, pressing a hand to his heart. He liked this woman more and more every minute. "I see I must endeavor to counter your cynicism."

Chelsa drew back, smiling in spite of herself. Those flashing white teeth and dimples were hard to resist. He was a man who liked to have fun and rarely took himself seriously. Oh, how she'd like to live such a carefree existence. But responsibilities and the nerve-racking edge of anticipation kept her feet on solid ground and her guard up.

"You could try," she said. "But every drop of that cynicism has been earned. The hard way."

The playful spark in his eyes turned serious. "I do not doubt that it has been earned. But it should not be so."

She had a hard time looking away from those penetrating dark eyes. There were deeper layers to Antonio Castillo that the headlines couldn't begin to uncover.

But Chelsa didn't have the luxury of plumbing those depths. Because the sooner he was out of their lives, the safer she and the girls would be.

He was way too visible. And she was doing her level best to be invisible.

"Perhaps I should call and notify someone of my whereabouts."

Chelsa went to the wall phone and lifted the receiver, then replaced it. "Phone's still out. You'd have a better idea than me of how fast your utility people move."

"About as swift as molasses. The islanders share a universal creed, I think. No one hurries."

"Will your family be worried?"

"They are not expecting me, no. And they rarely keep track of my comings and goings."

"You're kidding. With your status?"

"I told you, I am only the spare."

"Why do you do that?"

"What?"

"Discount your importance."

He shrugged. "It was not my intention to discount myself. It is simply a joke started when I was young and which I have carried over into adulthood."

She wondered if he'd carried it a bit too far, and if he did, indeed believe himself only an extra appendage to the royal family. "I guess my sense of humor's not up to speed these days."

"I would be happy to help you correct that." He waggled his eyebrows.

Unable to help it, she laughed. "Do you always joke around?"

"Always. Life is much too short to be glum. There are places to go, new experiences to be had, friends to make...*bellas* to woo."

She shook her head. The man was incorrigible. "I'll bet you've left a string of broken hearts across two continents."

"Ah, no. That would be bad of me. I am very careful not to cause heartache and strife. When I bid a woman *adiós,* it is with the knowledge that I have gained a new and lasting friendship."

Incredible as it seemed, she believed him. He had a gift for gab and a charm that wouldn't quit. His playful spirit wouldn't allow him to deliberately hurt someone. And she imagined he chose his companions based on the relativity scale of how they would handle a good time with no strings attached.

Although he managed to appear as though she had

his complete attention, his gaze kept straying to the window.

"There's not much left of your beautiful yacht that's salvageable."

He glanced back at her. "I noticed. Perhaps I could find a large enough piece to fashion a surfboard sail."

"I could help," Emily said.

"Me, too," Sophie chimed in, not one to be left out.

Chelsa, reaching for a mug, nearly knocked the ceramic in the sink. "You girls have lessons to do before you make any heavy plans." There. Certainly that was reasonable enough. She hadn't shouted, hadn't let loose the terror that nearly overwhelmed her every time she imagined her girls out of her sight. Vulnerable. A target of revenge.

"Aw, Momma."

"You know the rules. Now scoot."

Chairs scraped as they dutifully pushed away from the table and took their cereal bowls to the sink to be rinsed. Thank goodness for plastic. Sophie could barely reach the counter. As it was the bowl teetered on the edge of the tile before bouncing into the sink.

Once they were out of the room, Antonio gathered up his own dishes and tray. When he stood so close, naked beneath the flowery kimono, Chelsa's quivering insides went on high spin. And not from fear, this time.

"You are homeschooling Emily?"

"Yes. And Sophie, too, though she's not quite ready to start kindergarten."

"You are a teacher?"

"Was. My credentials are current, though. I got them through night school soon after Emily was born.'' Self-preservation, a means of something to fall back on. Rick had a tendency to gamble away his paycheck. When he was working that was.

''Now that I consider the matter, I realize the school term is not over yet for the summer. I had assumed you were on holiday.''

She hedged, not wanting to air the ugly details. The less said, the safer she was. However, his family did own the island of San Alegra. If he chose to dig, he could find out the whole story. ''We needed a change of scenery. I'm lucky that my writing and illustrating can be done from any location.''

''And that you have the qualifications to home-school your children should you decide to flee the country on a whim.''

''I rarely do anything on a whim.'' She got the feeling that his eyes saw way too much. And why had he said ''flee'' that way? For a moment, it looked as though he was going to press.

Then he reached past her, turning on the tap to rinse his dishes. His arm brushed her waist and she jumped aside as though she'd been goosed.

''You don't need to do the dishes.''

''I am capable. And you do not need to leap like a startled rabbit.''

''I didn't.''

''You did. Believe me, *bella,* when I make a move, you will know it.''

Her heart gave a slow, deep thud. ''Oh, please.''

He grinned, deliberately misunderstanding her mock sarcastic tone. ''It will be my pleasure. However, I find I must take a rain check. There are certain aches making themselves known in my body that would impede my concentration.'' He touched a finger to her lips. "And I imagine you are a woman who requires total concentration."

She shouldn't be standing here, allowing him to flirt, to touch her, to awaken her dormant hormones. But she couldn't seem to make herself move.

His gaze was fastened on her mouth.

"You carry the weight of the world on your shoulders, *querida*," he said softly, seriously. "Someone should pamper you." His lips brushed hers, a butterfly caress.

Warmth seeped through her, melting her heart, yet the fleeting touch was gone before it had ever really begun. He smelled like the sea and looked like a dream. The bruise on his forehead gave him a rakish air—much like a pirate—as did the dark hair that fell over his brow.

It took one hell of a man to look so incredibly virile while wearing a silky, feminine kimono sporting orange and fuchsia hibiscus.

But she suspected that Antonio Castillo was one hell of a man.

"Why did you do that?"

"Kiss you? Because you have a mouth made for loving. And it felt good."

Oh, this man could easily play with her heart.

And break it, if she wasn't careful.

"Just because something feels good, doesn't mean you should indulge. And I'd appreciate it if you wouldn't do it again."

"Ah, *querida*, I am thinking that I *will* do it again." He reached for a dish towel, dried his utensils and stacked the dishes neatly on the sideboard. "However, I will gallantly await an invitation."

"You'll have a long wait."

The light of challenge sparked in his dark, velvety eyes. "Patience is one of my finest virtues."

WHEN ANTONIO OPENED his eyes, it took him a minute to bring his recall into focus. The private stretch of beach had indeed been littered with debris. What remained of his yacht that hadn't ended up on shore had been washed out to sea, reduced to expensive floats for the gulls.

He'd found the slat inscribed with *Diablo Plata,* Silver Devil, intact and hauled it back to the screened-in porch of the bungalow. It was pitiful how that small amount of exercise had depleted his energy. Nausea welled and his head throbbed. Probably a concussion. Not his first, and more than likely, not his last. A lifestyle of courting danger ensured that.

Determined to restore his energy, he'd taken Chelsa's advice and returned to bed.

Now, with the late-afternoon sun slanting through the window, he was restless. *Dios,* he couldn't believe he'd slept around the clock. A first.

The bungalow was small, and he wondered who'd given up their sleeping quarters for him.

Chelsa, probably. There were traces of her here. Not many, but enough to recognize. Her citrus scent, for one, and a bottle of lotion on the dresser along with some hairpins and colored pencils. Since she didn't wear a lot of makeup, he assumed the latter was for illustrating her water babies series rather than painting her face. The other clue was the fact that her robe had been hanging on the door.

He heard childish whispers and looked toward the hallway. Raking his hair back off his forehead, he smiled and scooted up in the bed, testing his body parts. Still a little sore, but at least he no longer felt like a gored matador in a Barcelona bullring.

"Do not hide in the doorway, lovelies. Come in and keep me company."

The invitation caused a flurry of chatter and flying limbs and bouncing curls. He'd forgotten that children didn't *walk* or *sit* like normal people. They *landed*.

"Did you finish your lessons?"

"That was yesterday," Emily said.

"What a layabout I have become."

"No. Hurt people need rest to fix their bodies."

"Well, I feel properly fixed." He frowned when Sophie inched the covers off his chest. He wasn't too alarmed. He'd donned his jeans when they'd come out of the dryer and had fallen asleep with them on. "Have you lost something, little mermaid?"

"You didn't bleed."

She didn't have to sound so unhappy about it. "I am like a cat with many lives. I rarely bleed."

"I bleeded when Jimmy pushed me on the slide." She searched her knee, looking for evidence.

Emily rolled her eyes. "That was a long time ago, stupid."

Sophie sucked in a breath. "Ah-mmm. You're not s'posed to say 'tupid. Momma said. And it was so only millions and millions of days." This apparently meant fairly recent to a four-year-old.

Antonio figured he ought to intervene before there was mutiny and real bloodshed. Dutifully he ran his thumb over Sophie's baby-soft knee. Other than a few bruises here and there, there was no evidence of the dastardly slide incident.

"That was not at all charming of this Jimmy person

to push you. Shall I go sock him in the nose for you?''

Emily giggled, good humor restored. Ah, the resilience of kids.

But Sophie simply looked at him with wide, innocent eyes, contemplating. "Nope. Two wrongs doesn't make it right."

"Of course not. I lost my head for a moment."

"My grandpa lost his teeth."

He wasn't sure what one thing had to do with the other, but... "Did he find them?"

"Yep. They was in the glass. And they snapped like a mean old crocodile."

"Did not," Emily argued.

"Uh-huh! I seed it."

Highly entertained, Antonio laughed.

"How come grandpas get to take out their teeth?"

"Uh..." He searched for a plausible explanation. Kids asked the strangest questions. "I would say that's because they are special. When you live many many years, you learn fun tricks."

"Can you take yours out?"

Insulted, charmed, he chuckled. "I am not quite that old."

"How old are you?" Emily asked.

Keeping up with these little girls was like watching a fast and furious tennis match. "Twenty-nine." Vanity wouldn't let him admit that he'd be thirty in a matter of months—the expected age of marriage according to his mother, the queen. He shuddered.

"Momma's twenty-seven," Sophie volunteered. "She had a birfday. But it was spoiled when the policeman comed. 'Cept then we got to come here.

Momma said it was a late birfday party, a bee-u-te-ful vacation in Val—Vall…''

"Valldoria," he supplied.

"Yep."

The urge to pump these girls for information was strong. Antonio controlled the impulse, especially when he noticed how quiet Emily had become. Automatically he reached out and cupped her thin shoulder.

"You are lucky to have traveled to my country. It is indeed beautiful and I would be honored to act as your tour guide should you want to explore."

"We're not supposed to wander," Emily said quietly, shooting her sister a look that suggested she'd like to gag the four-year-old. Like her mother, this one took too many responsibilities on her slim shoulders.

"I gots seashells," Sophie announced, obviously unaware and uncaring that she'd switched subjects no less than six times in as many minutes. Without a care for his convalescence, she scrambled off the bed and charged out of the room, returning moments later to dump her cache on the quilt. Antonio only winced slightly when her foot landed on his sore stomach.

Not one to be outdone by her sister, Emily scooted closer. "If you don't be quiet, Momma's gonna come in," she scolded. Sophie slapped a hand over her mouth and glanced toward the door.

Antonio looked, too. He'd thought a lot about Chelsa Lawrence and was surprised by how much he wanted to see her, to drink in her scent, to touch her, to let her soft southern drawl wrap around him.

"Where is your mother?"

"Working. Even on vacations she gots deadlines."

"Her next installment of *The Adventures of Water Babies,* hum?"

"Uh-huh. Do your eyes hurt?"

Dios, he could hardly keep up. "No."

Sophie looked terribly disappointed.

"Why do you ask?"

"If your eyes hurted, I could tell you a story so you wouldn't have to read it."

He'd rather their mother tell him a story. One about policemen and vacations that were not as they seemed. The irregular pieces of this particular puzzle were beginning to worry him. After all, she was on Castillo land. If there was a possibility of danger, he should know about it.

However, at the moment, two little girls were waiting expectantly for his answer.

"Come to think of it, maybe they do hurt a bit. By all means, tell me a story."

"Well," Sophie brushed her hair out of her eyes and settled in. "There's this frog—"

"Naturally," Emily interrupted. "Because the water babies live in a pond and travel on the lily pads. Everybody knows frogs live by the pond, too."

Antonio nodded dutifully. Sophie, her wide round eyes that probably saw much more than anyone realized, suddenly inched up his chest and she poked a shy finger at his dimple.

"Did you used to be a frog and somebody kissed you and made you a prince?"

He grinned and held up a hand as if he were taking an oath. "I swear, I am only the spare. But the *real* prince—Joseph is his name—was most definitely an ugly old frog until beautiful Briana kissed him and laughed at him and yelled at him and he soon became a genuine prince.''

"Really?'' both girls sang.

"Really.''

"Who's Briana?''

"A lovely American who is the newest princess of my country.''

"And Joseph is your brother?''

"Yes. And he looks much more handsome being a happy prince rather than a sour old frog.''

Emily giggled. Sophie, however, seemed troubled.

She cupped her little hand over his jaw. "I'm jus' a mermaid. But my momma is very, very beautiful. I bet she could kiss you and make you into a real-life prince.''

The sound of Chelsa Lawrence's shocked gasp interrupted the offer.

Chapter Three

Chelsa was more than a little horrified. The thing about children was that you never knew what would come out of their mouths.

Antonio Castillo, bare-chested, with a huge, sexy-as-sin grin, was staring at her, the challenge in his dark eyes unmistakable.

Dear heaven, she couldn't wait for the phone lines to be fixed, couldn't wait out the week for the scheduled return of the ferry—the only way off the island.

She simply wouldn't make it.

"How about it, *querida*. Shall we conduct a test to see if your kiss is really magic?"

Oh, he thought he was so irresistible. Well, he was, but she certainly wasn't going to let on. She couldn't risk emotional involvement right now. Perhaps never.

"With the luck you've had recently, it'd probably backfire and you'd revert to a tadpole."

He shouted with laughter, and didn't even wince or hold his head.

"I see you're feeling better. Girls, go wash up so you can help me with dinner."

"Can we have hot dogs?"

"I hardly think that's a meal for company." For royalty.

"Don't bet on it," Antonio said. "That is the main staple at baseball games. We will simply pretend."

Chelsa was still hung up on those three words. *Bet on it.* Lord, she'd had her fill of that kind of talk.

"We're not at a game, and I've planned a civilized meal of barbecued chicken."

The girls grumbled.

"Ah, a picnic," Antonio inserted, changing the mood in an instant. The girls pounced.

"We could eat on a blanket!"

"And have a campfire!"

The conversation was fast getting out of control. She knew she couldn't keep her daughters sheltered inside the house forever. Perhaps if it were dark…

Antonio, studying her with shrewd eyes that continually astonished her—given that he was a carefree daredevil Casanova—saved her by intervening.

"Actually, *mi bellas,* I am still feeling a little weak from that unfortunate shipwreck and my foolish scavenger hunt across the beach when I was clearly not up to such activity. Perhaps we will save the blankets and sand for another time? The kitchen table is about as far as I can make it."

The girls went into instant sympathy mode. Chelsa felt grateful. And a little resentful. She'd had sole responsibility for these girls all their lives. Rick had never shown any interest. Now here was a rogue prince running interference, preventing squabbles and getting her daughters to fall right in line with barely a skirmish.

And to be honest, those squabbles were beginning to worry her. Emily and Sophie had taken to snipping at one another more lately than seemed normal. It tried her patience and played on her guilt.

Although she'd made every attempt to shield them as best she could, it was becoming heartbreakingly apparent that her best wasn't good enough.

"We could help you get to the table if you want," Emily said. "I have big muscles."

"Thank you, *diosa,* but I believe I can manage the distance."

Both girls nodded solemnly and filed out to do Chelsa's bidding.

Resentment faded, and in its place was something much more dangerous. If a woman wasn't scrupulously careful, she'd be hard-pressed not to fall for his charm and his looks—and his gentle way with her children.

Antonio Castillo got right down on their level, making them come alive in a way she hadn't seen since this whole ordeal with Rick had upended their lives.

He made Chelsa come alive, too, and that was even more terrifying. She'd made a big mistake in judgment once, and she was determined not to repeat it. She wasn't looking for a relationship, especially with someone as high-profile as Antonio Castillo—not that she was in the least suitable for the consort of a prince.

Lost in thought, she hadn't realized he'd gotten out of bed. His warmth invaded her senses first, then his scent, masculine, clean, like the allure of a seductive ocean breeze. The gentle touch of his hand on her shoulder, then softly in her hair caused her to whirl around with a jerk.

"Easy, *querida.*"

"Sorry."

"For what? A mother's worry? They are wonderful children. And resilient. They will be fine."

"How do you know? You know nothing about us."

"This may be so. But I would like to. I cannot help but respond when I see distress."

"I'm not distressed."

"And you are also not a very good liar."

She closed her eyes against the weight pressing in on her. She'd yearned for only a few things in life— family, commitment, honesty.

Safety.

She had the family. The rest had fallen apart.

"Talk to me," he said softly. "Perhaps I can help."

Oh, she wished that he could. Like a fairy tale, he could sweep her up, turn her world into a magical place of stardust and moonbeams, where happily-ever-after was a given.

But her life wasn't a fairy tale. And this particular prince would only cause more harm. Inadvertently, to be sure, but a fact nonetheless.

"Thank you for your concern, but we're fine." She turned to go.

"Chelsa?"

"Yes?"

"If it makes a difference, the queen places high importance on my ability to impart advice. It is fairly ridiculous in my opinion, but who am I to question a queen?"

"Or your mother?"

"That, too."

She smiled. "I like you, Antonio Castillo."

"That is an excellent start. And soon, I believe, you will like me so much, you will begin to call me Tony."

She felt her eyelids go heavy, felt her stomach give a giddy leap. "Maybe I will." Astonished, she realized she was on the verge of flirting.

And it felt entirely too good.

THE EVENING MEAL was light and delicious. He'd dined with movie stars and royalty, in glamorous settings and sparkling cities. Yet the simple table set for four in a small island bungalow, where children switched subjects faster than any sane person could keep up, and a delicate Southern belle presided like a born socialite, taking the chaos in stride, was somehow more stimulating than he'd ever experienced.

While Chelsa went through the ritual of putting her daughters to bed, Antonio wandered the rooms. There were drawing boards, sketch pads and computer apparatus lying about, the tools of Chelsa's trade. He picked up the sketchbook and grinned at the half-finished drawings of frogs depicting various states of emotion, spiders wearing bow ties and fish twirling in stiff net tutus.

Curious, he thumbed through the published copies of the books the girls had told him about.

She wrote under the name of Rose O'Mally.

The animated characters appealed to his sense of fun, and he chuckled. Obviously Chelsa Lawrence shared that sense of fun. Otherwise she would not have been able to create such magical whimsy.

Yet to look into her lake-blue eyes, one would never know she possessed such a delightful streak. She harbored secrets and the crushing weight of responsibilities. There were fears, barely leashed, and a distinct hesitation over every move or decision.

Not the characteristic of a creator of fancy.

Intrigued, he eased onto the sofa, wincing only slightly when his ribs protested, and was thoroughly captivated by the tale that unfurled.

The story was about a water baby—a frog naturally, he remembered Emily saying—being scared by a bad spider. But the spider was scared of the water. Nobody liked the spider because he was hairy and ugly, and because nobody liked him, he was lonely and sad and he cried. So the baby finally looked past the ugly exterior and extended a lily pad for the spider to sit on and float. The spider was happy and became friends with the water baby, and the moral was not to be mean to people because they look different or because somebody else says they bite. Give a chance and be sweet to everybody.

"Did it hold your interest?" Chelsa asked from the doorway.

His gaze lifted, met hers and held. Soft lamplight created a halo backdrop for her wheat-blond hair, giving her the look of an angel. His savior angel. So sweet and poised, yet full of contradictions. "I was riveted. You tend to put different spins on the same themes. Morality and honesty."

She shrugged. "I suppose because they're important to me. I try to instill those qualities in my daughters."

"And in the process, you teach millions of other children the same lessons."

"The world could use a little more morals and honesty. For some it's too late. Catch them while they're young and perhaps we'll make an impact."

"A worthy goal. So why do you not take credit by writing under your own name?"

Now they were treading on shaky ground. "It's not uncommon to take a pseudonym."

"In the event of fame and fortune?"

She smiled evasively. "I'll leave the fame stuff to you. You're so good at it."

"I have fun, yes. But we were speaking of you. Is the writing of children's books a lucrative one?"

"For me it is. I don't make a fortune, but I'm comfortable. The series took off practically overnight and at times I'm hard-pressed to keep up. In fact, I'm terribly behind right now because the girls are so intrigued by San Alegra. They've never seen the ocean before and they'd stay outdoors twenty-four hours if I'd let them. Makes it tough to maintain any kind of regular work schedule."

"Perhaps I could assist you there. Since the ferry won't be here for another week, and my yacht is in pieces, I will need to go into town and purchase some essentials. I would be happy to take the girls with me, allow them to explore, and in turn allow you some time to yourself."

"No." She twisted her hands, lowered her voice. "Thank you, but no. The girls can be a handful and I don't like to impose."

He frowned at her obvious agitation. "It is not imposing when an offer has been extended."

Her smile, though strained, inched up. "If you had any idea what you'd be getting into, you wouldn't extend it in the first place. I'm saving your sanity."

She was holding something back, but he decided to let her off the hook. For the moment. "There are those who say my sanity has already snapped."

"There is that," she said, her features easing. "I've read about you, you know. You court danger like it's nothing more that a leisurely Sunday drive. Race cars, motorcycles, boats. The journalists say you're fearless."

"Ah, no. Not in everything."

"What are you afraid of?"

"My mother," he said immediately. Then more thoughtfully, "Southern women whose souls speak so loudly through their eyes."

She glanced away.

"What are you running from, *querida?*"

"Nothing."

He rose, took both her hands in his. They trembled, he noticed. And that wariness was flashing in her eyes. "You can trust me."

"My ability to trust was lost long ago. Besides, I don't even know you."

"I am an open book—ask anyone." He gave her fingers a gentle, encouraging squeeze. "Are you in trouble?"

"No."

"Then why do you panic when I suggest you or your daughters accompany me outside?"

Chelsa pulled her hands away and wrapped her arms around her waist. She didn't want to air her dirty laundry, but she felt she had little choice. She'd made a decision to rescue this man, and felt responsible for him. Although she could ask him to relocate to a hotel in town, there would be nothing stopping him from coming back to visit, whether to see her girls, who were already half in love with him, or to canvas the sand for strewn parts of his yacht.

And because of who he was, he would put them in danger.

She had to make him understand this.

Letting out a resigned breath, she looked out the darkened windows where a million stars twinkled like magical diamonds above the sea. The lulling, rhythmic sound of surf meeting sand should have soothed. Yet her stomach was twisted in knots.

"In a way, I guess you could say I'm a fugitive. But I'm not running from the law. I'm running from the screwed-up system the law's become." She glanced at him, braced herself. "Sophie told you her daddy is in jail. I put him there."

His gaze sharpened, searching.

She read his thoughts before he could even voice them. "No, no scars. Yet." Feeling exposed, she drew the curtains closed, fisting the delicate fabric, shutting out the bogeyman. "He didn't beat me. He beat the system."

"How?"

"International fraud. He sold Mississippi mud to unsuspecting folks, convincing them they were investing in an up-and-coming, affordable resort. Senior citizens turned over their life savings and couples raided their nest eggs and children's college funds in order to invest. Rick was a gambler, always looking for a way to make an easy buck. He was charming and slick and dishonest as the day is long."

She let go of the curtains, found she didn't know what to do with her empty hands, so she crossed them at her waist, holding on, wishing desperately that for once there was another set of arms besides her own to hold her, to protect her.

But wishes were for fairy tales and the pages of her books.

"At first I closed my eyes to what was going on. We married young and had the girls right away. I thought I had the perfect family, the perfect life. But soon after Sophie was born, something changed in Rick. What I'd always passed off as moodiness gradually escalated into nastiness. He became paranoid and suspicious, and tried to put that blame off on me. For a while I took it, until I realized that my misery was affecting the children." The shame of being such a stupid, blind doormat still had the power to sting.

"Then the late-night disappearances began. He started wearing a pager and it went off at all hours of the day and night."

"Where did he go when he left?"

"He'd rented a room outside of town, and a telephone. That's where he did his betting and his telemarketing to fleece trusting individuals out of their savings. He used our household money to bet on everything from horses to armadillo races. I never saw any of the money he swindled with those phony property deeds. He banked it overseas."

"Did none of these people think to check out what they were purchasing?"

She could understand his incredulous tone, but he didn't know Rick, didn't know his slick manner. "Evidently he sent phony pictures, and held people off from coming by telling them he would arrange prepaid travel for a groundbreaking ceremony."

"Were there others involved?"

"A couple of young kids he'd hired to make calls. As it turns out, they didn't know it was a scam. But somebody must have caught on." She'd never seen such a serious, fierce expression on Antonio Castillo's face. She almost liked it better when he was grinning like a spoiled, obscenely rich second son of a king with nothing more on his mind than the next adventure. The handsome man standing before her, though, was proving there were deeper layers beneath the carefree mask he showed the world.

For some reason, that depth scared her, made her realize this was a man she could easily fall for. And *that,* she could not do.

"We lived in a small town in Mississippi, and people began to notice the changes in Rick. I made excuses for him until the day the detective showed up at my door and told me they suspected him of being involved in a fraud scam. For a while they suspected me, too."

"You were investigated?"

She nodded. "Thankfully my father was a retired police officer, and that went a long way to giving me credibility. I started divorce proceedings and set a trap. I was instrumental in putting him in jail."

"And the money? Was it recovered?"

"Some of it." She shrugged. "The rest, I don't know. Maybe he blew it on gambling." She closed her eyes, shoved at her hair with her hands. "I feel so guilty, like I should make restitution to those people."

Dios, this woman carried a lot. And her sense of honesty and fairness would make her want to pay from her own pockets. Antonio made a mental note to dig deeper into the case, to add his own funds to the pot if it were indeed dry.

"What was your husband's prison term?"

"Not nearly long enough. Slick lawyers have a

way of getting reduced sentences. Then there's time off for good behavior.'' She made a disgusted sound.

"His behavior has not been good?"

"Oh, the prison officials don't see him as bad. They claim he's a model jailhouse citizen, totally repentant for his misdeeds.''

He frowned, feeling a sense of foreboding at her tone. "You are not only speaking of the fraud, I think.''

"No. He swore to get even with me. To make me pay.''

"Dios.''

"Exactly, and he's up for parole. If he's freed, I become a prisoner.'' She pinned him with a steady look.

"Do you understand now, Tony?'' In her agitation, she didn't appear aware that she'd used his name. "Because of who you are, you could put us in danger. You're recognizable worldwide. Even Rick followed your racing career like a demented fan. Tabloids snap your picture if you so much as step out a door. Sports enthusiasts and social columnists speculate over and document your every move—and those of whoever happen to be standing next to you. I can't allow my daughters to be in the limelight like that. I can't take the chance on Rick finding us.''

"How serious of a threat are we talking about here?''

"About as serious as it gets. He wants me dead.''

"¡Madre de Dios!'' Her stark statement stole his breath. He was a man who laughed at death, challenged it even.

But that was him. The thought of threat or harm

befalling Chelsa Lawrence and her children was intolerable.

"Why are you here alone?" he demanded. "Why are you not under police protection?"

"Because there's no evidence of intent. Only the whispered words of a convict just before he was taken away in chains."

He had to get a grip, yet it was difficult to think clearly past the rage that roiled inside him. She was so delicate, so beautiful, so genuine. She didn't deserve this strife. "Perhaps he has had a change of heart."

She shook her head. "I saw his eyes, Tony. And I won't gamble with my children's future on the off chance that he's had a sudden attack of remorse."

"Are you in contact with the officials? Will you know if the parole board frees him?"

"Detective D'Ambra is keeping tabs, and he's promised to call and let me know what happens. Mitch is the one who arranged for us to come here."

"Mitch?"

"D'Ambra. The detective. He trained with a man named Cole Martinez, and when this case came up, they worked on it together. You see, Rick didn't limit himself to fleecing only Americans. He branched out internationally."

Which gave the Castillos jurisdiction if Lawrence showed up in their country. *Smart man, this D'Ambra,* Antonio thought. Because, in Valldoria, they handled felons differently, had less red tape to cut through.

"Cole is one of my closest friends," he said. "Is he still on the case?"

"That's just it. There *is* no case. Only the panic of an ex-wife."

She said it self-deprecatingly, but he didn't believe it for a moment. Chelsa Lawrence might be delicately built, only reaching as far as his chin—and that was stretching it—but she had a backbone that was amazing. They bred them strong in the South. The poise and manners were deceiving, though. This wasn't a woman who'd be blown away by a gust of wind.

Nor would she panic at nothing.

Admiration warred with his protective instincts. He had an idea she had a core of strength that just might outmatch his. Still, he had connections. And he knew how to evade the press, knew how to become invisible.

"I do not believe it is possible for you to overreact."

"Thank you," she said, her eyes meeting his with both relief and reserve. "But whether or not I'm fabricating the whole thing, I'm going to have to ask you to leave."

He shook his head, stepped closer, cupped her cheek. He'd thought he knew all there was to know about women, but with Chelsa, he realized he would have to learn all over again. This woman was wounded. Oh, she hid it well, but the wound was there, and it cut deep.

And he was attracted to her in a way he couldn't quite define.

But playboy innuendos and whirlwind affairs wouldn't work with her. Nor would a sophisticated one-night stand. This was a woman who needed a slow touch, an easy touch. A woman who needed the security of a guy who had staying power, not one who lived in fear of moss growing under his feet.

Nevertheless his hero's heart kicked in. The need to take care of her was fierce, blocking out all else.

He ran his thumb over her soft jaw. "You need someone to lean on. And I have broad shoulders."

"I can't—"

He placed a finger over her lips. "You are in my country now—or at least on Castillo land. It is both my obligation and my pleasure to see that you come to no harm."

Chapter Four

Chelsa stepped back from his touch. The timing was so inappropriate for her to react to his masculinity, to his velvety eyes that radiated sincerity and a sex appeal so strong, it nearly brought her to her knees.

"Weren't you listening to me?" she demanded.

"To every word."

"Then you've got to know that staying with me is impossible."

"If we were in Mississippi, perhaps. Here, we are in my territory. I know these people. I know their loyalties and their creeds."

"Their loyalties to you?"

"Yes. This island is small, and though tourism is important, the locals do not actively pursue it. They would be as upset as you with a media circus."

"I doubt it." Her words rang with unresolve. He still didn't understand. And why would he? Being the center of attention was a way of life to him, a given.

But that wasn't a life-style most normal people lived. And because she was one of those everyday type of souls, she felt like she was the wiser one on the subject.

"It was not my intention to discount your feelings,

querida. Let us agree that your reasons for anonymity and the town's are vastly different. Yet you would be surprised at the ally they represent.''

"How can you be sure?''

"I have grown up in and around here. My appearance or presence does not cause the citizens to go into a dither. They respect my privacy because I am one of their own.''

"And your family owns the island,'' she inserted. "Let's don't forget that.''

"Ownership is not an issue among friends.''

He seemed so certain. "What about tourists? Maybe they're not so common, but there are bound to be some.''

"And they are just that. People enjoying a vacation. You are becoming paranoid to think they would run immediately to the telephones to notify the press.''

The word *paranoid* stung. She turned, pushed through the screen door and walked out into the night, the sand cool beneath her bare feet. The windows remained open, so she could hear the girls if they woke up. She needed a minute to herself, to steady her emotions.

But she wasn't permitted that moment. A soft touch at her shoulder had her jumping.

"Easy,'' Antonio murmured. "Just me.''

Her nerves were screaming, and she was almost afraid to open her mouth and speak. No telling what would come out. She wanted to lash out at someone— anyone—and Antonio was the closest. But the mess she was in wasn't his fault.

She took a breath, reached deep for calm. "Maybe I am overreacting, but I'm scared. If that makes me paranoid in your eyes, then I'm sorry." For reasons she didn't want to get into, it upset her that this man would think her weak. She wanted to make an impression on him. A good one.

Which was silly, really. He was a prince. She was just a small-town Mississippi mother on the run. She'd never been to Hollywood, or gone sailing, or attended a Grand Prix or a bullfight. She'd never met anyone who had celebrity status and wouldn't know the first thing about his world.

Her world revolved around her daughters and writing children's books. Nothing fancy about that.

He slid his hand beneath her hair and touched the nape of her neck, gently, the butterfly caress raising chills along her arms.

"Ah, sweet Chelsa. I have again misspoken and wounded you. It is I who shall apologize." His fingers kneaded her shoulders, his breath warm against her ear. "I am not judging you poorly. In my blundering way I am merely asking you to trust me."

"Said the spider to the fly," she muttered. She felt the length of him against her back. He was a man who touched and held as though it was second nature. A woman could read more into his instinctive actions and attentiveness than was safe.

And safety was definitely an issue right now.

"No, *querida,* I am not attempting to catch you in my web. I may be irresponsible at times, but I am not deceitful."

She shouldn't continue to allow him to hold her like this, with his hands at her shoulders and his virile body brushing hers, but she couldn't seem to move. The sand beneath her feet might as well have been quicksand.

"I didn't think Rick was deceitful, either."

"Of course not. But will you judge all others by his behavior? Is that the message you would pass on to your little girls? Your animated water babies extend friendship to others. Can you not practice what you preach?"

"A fictional story is a far cry from real life."

"Perhaps. But a part of you comes across in those pages. I am attempting to extend to you my friendship. All you have to do is reach out and accept it."

"At one time that might have been easy. Now, though..." She shook her head. "How do you really trust someone, Tony?"

Suddenly the warmth of his body left her. Confused, she watched as he moved in front of her, his back to her, and glanced over his shoulder. Holding his arms straight out from his sides, he said, "It is simple. Catch me."

"Wait!" She muffled an astonished laugh when he started to sway backward. "You're kidding, right?"

"No. I am serious. Catch me."

"I can't. You're too big. You'll get hurt, and I'm not going to be responsible for a second concussion on top of the one you probably already have." She glanced at the sand. He wouldn't crack his head open, but still. "And it's not that simple."

"Yes. It is *just* that simple. I trust you not to let me fall."

"That's ridiculous. You don't know—" Her words halted abruptly. Without warning he leaned back... and back. Good night, he was going to do it!

She leapt forward, hooked her arms beneath his and barely had time to link her fingers over his chest before she was accepting his weight, holding him, going down to the soft packed sand with him in her arms, breaking his fall.

Panting, her hip jarred slightly from the fall, she lightly punched his chest. "You idiot! You could have hurt yourself."

"No. You would not let that happen."

"How do you know?"

"Because I know you."

She made a disbelieving sound deep in her throat. "What if I'd turned my back at the last minute?" Somebody ought to put this man in a straitjacket for his own good.

His teeth flashed white in his too-handsome face. "But you didn't. Just like you didn't turn your back when I required rescuing from the surf."

"I thought about it," she muttered. "I didn't know who was on that yacht."

"But in the end you made the choice, at the risk of peril to yourself. That says more about you than you realize."

"You're giving me too much credit. Sophie and Emily put a guilt trip on me. Otherwise I'd have just gone back in the house."

"Then my gratitude goes to your sweet daughters, as well. However, I believe you are fibbing."

"I don't fib."

"You did just now." Again his sexy smile flashed. "White lies are forgivable on occasion."

She realized she was holding him in her arms. Her breasts were pressed against his back, his silky dark hair brushing her chin as he gazed up at her. Just like a lover. Intimately. Oh, he did that so well. Her legs were spread wide, cradling his hips, making her yearn.

And that yearning was out of the question.

She pushed at him, and he sat up. Crossing her legs, she sifted sand through fingers that trembled like an addict coming off drugs.

He faced her, mirroring her position, and touched the back of her knuckles. "Shall we reverse roles now?"

He was asking more than she could give. Blind trust. An absolute folly. He was watching her closely, waiting. The smell of the sea and the rhythmic ebb and flow of waves should have lulled her. In a perfect world this setting would invite soft whispers and confidences. Romance even.

But there wasn't room in her life for whispers or romantic interludes. Only for sick dread and nerve-shattering anticipation.

White foam glittered in the light of the moon, but beyond the shoreline was only vast darkness. Although the balmy breeze held no chill, she shivered.

Across that ocean—somewhere—there was an unstable man who could make the world believe he was an innocent lamb, when in fact he was a nasty, devious, rabid wolf.

"Sometimes we think we know someone, but we really don't. I didn't know Rick."

"We are all entitled to make mistakes."

"Mine was a doozy." Absently she trailed her fingers through the sand, drawing animated stick figures that would be washed away when the tide came in.

"Was there ever a time when you could count on your husband?"

She didn't have a ready answer. Maybe at first. Maybe not at all. She shrugged.

"Did he ever promise not to let you fall?" he pressed.

"No...I never asked."

"Will you ask me?"

He said it so softly, his Latin accent washing over her like the thrilling caress of a welcome breeze. She didn't understand his persistence. This was a man reputed to get itchy feet when he stayed in one place too long, spent too much time with one woman. "Why?"

"Because you never ask anything of others. You take it all on your shoulders. You did not trust your husband, even if it was a subconscious mistrust. You earned your teaching degree to have something to fall back on. You wrote your books, yet hid behind the name of another. Why was that?"

"Because he gambled." Her head jerked up. Antonio had a way of lulling her into admissions she didn't mean to impart. She sighed. "I wanted desperately to stay at home with my children, and that's why I toyed with the idea of writing. I had to work because I needed money for groceries, for the girls' clothes, for the rent."

She pushed her hair back from her face. "When I was offered the contract for the water babies series, it was like a dream come true. I nearly told him...." She rubbed her palms on her knees, feeling pitiful that a wife could not tell her own husband of her success. "You guessed right. In the end I hid it from him, let him believe it was just a hobby. He wasn't home all that much anyway, so it was fairly easy."

"And why did you feel the need to hide?"

"If he'd seen the checks, he would have squandered the money, wanting to invest it in his next get-rich scheme.''

"He would have stolen from you and his children.''

"No—''

"Yes. It is the same thing.''

He was right. And it made her feel ashamed that she'd married a man who was like that, allowed him to hoodwink her so.

"I have an obscene amount of money,'' he said, causing her to take a mental step back in order to catch up. "I would ask nothing of you…except for one thing.''

The skepticism that reared its ugly head was unavoidable. "What?''

"That you trust me with your friendship.'' He got to his feet, pulled her up with him and stepped behind her. "No, do not turn or look at me.''

She did anyway, glancing over her shoulder, confused and wary.

His elevated brows told her he understood how difficult it was for her, that he was prepared to give her slack—to a point.

"Fall back, *querida*. I will catch you.''

His patience, and his utterly sincere, trustworthy look caused a chink in her armor. "You're too far away. If I did decide to play this silly game—and I haven't yet made up my mind—you'd have to come closer.''

He shook his head. "This is far from a game, *bella*. Trust that I will be there when it matters.''

"I can't,'' she whispered. Her voice trembled and she straightened her spine against the weakness.

"Yes, you can. Do it.''

She hesitated, thinking about it. She was nuts. Truly, certifiably nuts, yet a small part of her wanted to prove something.

Actually, more like a really big part of her. She hadn't always been so cynical. At one time she'd been vibrant, full of joy, looking forward to each new day and experience. Was that same woman who'd looked at the world through rose-colored glasses still inside her?

"If you let me fall, you've had it."

He tisked. "And ruin my sterling reputation? Never. Come on, Chelsa."

The rush of adrenaline made her dizzy as she vacillated back and forth between courage and cowardice. She started to raise her arms out to her sides, then hesitated.

He sighed. "Have your girls never leapt from a high place and expected you to catch them?"

Her arms faltered. "Yes. What kid hasn't?"

"And did you catch them?"

"Of course I did. But that's different. I'm their mother."

"It is the same principle, Chelsa."

She didn't think so. And doggone it, his voice sounded even farther away. She started to turn her head.

"No. Do not look. Just leap."

"That's so totally irresponsible."

"I am not asking you to be irresponsible. We are conducting a test, a lesson. Show me that steel I know is running through your backbone, Ms. Lawrence."

Well, he certainly knew how to push her buttons. Her arms whipped right out to her sides as though they'd been jerked by a puppeteer at a children's party.

Her heart pounded and her palms grew slick. The doubting voice inside her told her this wasn't going to work.

"Come closer."

"Trust me, *bella*. When you need me, I will be close enough. You have my word. Fall back."

She closed her eyes, and gathered her nerve. Arms out to her sides, she leaned back. Blood rushed to her head, adrenaline shot through her and the world spun.

For a split second she felt herself free-falling.

Then terror swamped her, catching her off guard like a monster rising out of a green mist.

She didn't want to play.

He was the daredevil. Not her. This wasn't a sure thing, and she'd learned to avoid anything that wasn't an absolute. She wanted to call it off.

He wouldn't make it in time, he was too far away.

But she was past the point of no return, too late to stop the momentum, too late to even bend her legs and break the fall.

She opened her mouth to scream, yet her lungs shut down. Time ground to a halt, like a freeze frame on a VCR videotape. As though trapped in a surrealistic world of distorted images, her peripheral vision sharpened. Powdery Mediterranean sand rushed up to meet her in excruciatingly slow motion.

Every muscle in her body knotted in anticipation of impact, of pain. And oh, she knew about pain, the tearing of a dream, the shredding of insides, of a heart. In a mere fraction of a second, that pain would radiate to encompass a bruised body, too.

Strong arms slid under her, banded around her.

The world tilted as Antonio broke her fall, swept her up into his arms and cradled her close to his chest.

"Shh. I've got you, *querida*."

She wasn't even aware of the tears that trickled down her face until he ran his lips over the salty tracks. Her heart thundered in her ears.

She felt like a fool.

And she felt like the most cherished woman on earth.

He sat with her, held her there in the sand, stroked her hair and ran his thumb beneath her eyes, over her cheeks.

She looked up at him, expecting teasing triumph. What she saw was something else entirely. Intensity. Seriousness. Compassion.

And desire.

That last emotion registered an instant before his lips covered hers. Softly. Oh, so softly.

Her body went limp, melting into his, meeting the kiss and reveling in it. It had been so long, so very long since she'd felt so cherished, so safe. Her mind went blank of every responsibility she had, of every worry.

The smell of the sea and the man wrapped around her like a comforting cocoon. Yet comfort wasn't in any way the right description for what he made her feel. She curled in his lap, feeling his arms tighten around her. Her own arms went around his neck, her fingers delving into his hair.

He kissed her with an expertise that stole her breath. The scratch of his whiskers on her face would leave marks, but she couldn't think about that now. She could only feel. Heat, flashing and incendiary, whipped through her.

Her ankle-length sundress had ridden up on her legs, and she felt his hand at her thigh, burning through the cotton, his fingers stroking the sensitive skin just beneath the raised hem.

With a verve she'd repressed for way too long, she angled into the kiss, urging him to take it deeper, to take her higher.

Maybe it was her own hungry moan, or maybe it was the rogue wave crashing against the rocks that finally penetrated her sensual web, startling her. Reluctance was keen, but she managed to pull back.

Feeling drugged, her nerve endings ultrasensitive, she lifted her head and met the sensual gleam in his dark eyes.

Good night, what in the world had possessed her to allow things to go this far? She had an idea she wouldn't soon forget this man's touch, his taste. And like a coveted dream just out of reach, it would haunt her nights and her days.

"You said you'd wait for an invitation," she whispered. His palm was like a sensual brand against her thigh. A warm ocean breeze licked over her exposed skin that hummed with exquisite stimulation. A stimulation so heightened, it bordered on pain.

"Yes. And your expressive eyes have given it." He stared at her for so long, searching. "Do you deny it?"

No, she couldn't. She straightened and untangled herself from his lap, feeling a little bereft when he let her go so easily. If she didn't know better, she'd imagine he was as shell-shocked as she.

Which was a ridiculous fancy. This was a worldly man, used to casual encounters. It showed just how far out of his league she was that she should read more into a look, or a touch, than was there.

Trying for a modicum of sophistication, she said, "Your reputation is well earned. You pack quite a kiss, Prince Antonio."

He winced. "Ah, *querida,* I had not expected you to toss reputation and hearsay in my face."

"Are you saying it's unwarranted?"

His look was unreadable. "Depends on which part we're discussing."

"I think you know."

His dimples flashed. "I court danger, yes. And I love women. But I am not the carousing tomcat you might think."

"Well…" She didn't know what to say. Suddenly she felt embarrassed by her own passionate part in the kiss. She'd pounced on him like a starving woman at a feast. Pathetic.

Nerves zinging, she twisted her hands, then ran her damp palms down the sides of her dress and cleared her throat. "It's late. I should check on the girls and go to bed."

The minute she voiced the intention, another wave of heat suffused her body. If she didn't force her feet to move, she was going to do something stupid. Like invite him to join her.

His sexy grin told her he knew exactly what she was thinking. Squaring her shoulders, she returned the grin, feigning a savoir faire she was far from feeling, and blew him a kiss. "In your dreams, Prince." She turned to go in the house.

"Chelsa?"

She paused, keeping her back to him. Otherwise he would see her desire, see her for the fraud she was, see that it was taking every shred of good sense she possessed to keep from extending her hand...and begging. "Yes?"

"You are already in my dreams. Where would you like me to sleep?"

She whipped around. Darn him for being such a mind reader. "What—"

"Apparently I have appropriated your bed, and I am much too gallant to put you out of it two nights in a row. Although I find the idea of sharing a bed with you highly appealing, I do not think that is what you had in mind." His smile was boyish, his dark brows raised in apparent innocence. "So that I do not overstep my welcome, where would you like me to retire?"

With me was not an acceptable reply. And his gallantry created a problem. Last night she'd bunked with the girls since the sofas in the front room were actually a grouping of love seats, not nearly big enough to stretch out on. And if they were too small for her, there was no way they'd accommodate Antonio's six-foot-plus frame.

Of course, there was always the hammocklike glider on the porch, but that still offended her sense of hospitality. One did not banish a prince to the porch.

Where was a decent etiquette book when you needed it? In deference to his title, she should be the one to sleep on the porch, and she might have if it didn't make her feel so vulnerable.

She needed locked doors made of solid wood, not a mere screen with a flimsy latch.

He seemed to fall in with her thoughts. "Perhaps I should take the cushions on the porch?"

"No. That wouldn't be—"

"I do not require palatial accommodations if that is what you are thinking. Many of my nights are spent on the deck of my yacht, under the stars. The glider will feel like a luxurious featherbed compared to the unyielding teak."

"That's not it." She hedged. "You'd end up being locked out. What if you had to, um, get up to go to the bathroom, or something?"

Antonio watched her nervousness. Yes, she would lock the interior door, because she was afraid. And rightly so. The more he thought about it, the more he decided he should sleep on the porch. To stand guard.

A damsel in distress would bring out his protective instincts every time. Usually he could fix the problem with money. In this case, or a least at the moment, he couldn't.

"Perhaps you could give me the key. That way, if I require entrance, I will not wake you."

"I don't know... You're a guest."

"An uninvited one. I will not abuse your hospitality by putting you out of your bed." He didn't think now was a good time to tell her he'd like to be in that bed *with* her. "The porch will be fine, *querida.*"

She nodded. "I'll leave the key out, then."

He watched her walk to the bungalow, transfixed by the graceful sway of her body, by the way the moonlight glowed off her wheat-colored hair. The humid, salt air had turned it into a mass of springy curls that brushed her shoulders and back. His own fingers had contributed to the disarray.

He rubbed a hand over his chest, feeling a strange ache just beneath his breastbone. He licked his lips, tasting her there. The citrus scent of her perfume lingered in his senses; even the soft ocean breeze swirling around him couldn't erase the smell of her, the feel of her.

¡Dios! He didn't like to admit it, but that kiss had scared the hell out of him. He'd courted many woman, shared deep intimacies with some—though not nearly as many as the media would have the world think—but he'd never experienced a reaction quite like this one.

Raking his hair back from his face, he kept his gaze on the house, saw her go inside, then slip back out, obviously putting the key on the wicker table for him. He saw her hesitate, searching the darkness for him.

The interior lights created a halo backdrop behind her, and his heart gave a funny lurch, surprising him. He was used to the rush of adrenaline as he pushed an Indy car to its limits or soared through the sky piloting his own Learjet.

What he felt looking at Chelsa Lawrence, kissing her, was something else entirely.

She'd tasted just like his destiny.

And that shook him up.

He wasn't a man who wandered aimlessly through life, searching for what he wanted to be when he grew up. Antonio knew exactly what his destiny was—to enjoy the freedom of being a rolling stone, to experience life to its fullest, to never settle in one place long enough for the possibility of boredom to set in, for the walls to crowd in and smother him.

His life was dedicated to the pursuit of having fun.

The lights in the bungalow winked off, and Antonio let out a breath he hadn't realized he'd been holding.

It was utterly foolish to think that a kiss could taste

like destiny. Obviously he was not yet recovered from the bump on the head.

And furthermore, he lectured himself, Chelsa Lawrence was not a woman a man could toy with. As much as she insisted she could stand on her own, she had *commitment* stamped all over her. In bold letters.

And if there was one thing Antonio was allergic to, it was commitment.

So why, then, was his heart pulsing like a high-performance piston in an engine revved past the red line?

Chapter Five

Chelsa could tell by the slant of the sun shining through the bedroom window that she'd overslept. Tossing back the sheet, she jumped out of bed, taking a moment to overcome the vertigo of the swift move, then stumbled into the bathroom across the hall to wash her face.

She'd already crossed the threshold before the voices registered in her foggy brain.

Those excited voices, and the sight before her, brought her suddenly, shockingly awake.

Antonio stood at the pedestal sink, razor poised in hand. White lather covered his cheeks, contrasting with his golden skin and dark hair. His only concession to modesty was the ivory towel wrapped around his waist.

Good night, this man was lethal.

The part of her brain that managed to function noted that Emily and Sophie were perched on the toilet, watching the masculine ritual with avid glee. Surely that wasn't appropriate...

"Good morning, *querida*."

Stunned, unable to find her voice, she dragged her gaze from his impressive chest and bare legs. Feeling like a total coward, she avoided looking directly at his face, and instead glanced fully at her daughters....

And at the scrawny black and white cat Sophie was hugging.

"Where did you get that cat?"

"He got scared in the storm. We finded him when we went to get seashells and Antonio's toothpicks."

Toothpicks? Oh, the wreckage of the boat, she realized. Then the words sank in. "You went outside without my permission?" She knew her voice had risen, but she couldn't help it.

Sophie's arms tightened around the cat and it yowled.

Antonio paused, razor poised to swipe another furrow down his lean cheek, his gaze meeting hers in the mirror. "They were with me."

Trust me. His eyes said it; not his mouth. She felt like a ninny.

"Can we keep him, Momma?" Emily asked, reaching over Sophie's shoulder to pet the animal.

"I don't know, hon. He's probably someone's pet."

"Nuh-uh!" Sophie said. "He was lost and scared and he gots nobody but us."

Chelsa caught herself looking at Antonio for help. Dear Lord, she'd never done that before. She'd had sole responsibility for her daughters, been the only decision maker since Emily was born. So why had she slipped into that beseeching role?

Before she could correct the error, Antonio had wiped away the remaining shaving cream and turned to face her.

"We can call the information center in town and place an inquiry."

It was a good suggestion. Chelsa just wished he'd kept his back turned while he made it. Facing her as he was, her imagination took off in a major flight of erotic fancy at the sight of the gap in the towel. The terry cloth was only held up by an overlapping of material. One false move and they'd all get an interesting peep show.

And while she would secretly enjoy the show, her wide-awake brain decided this was *not* an appropriate setting for the girls.

"That's a good idea," she said, silently cursing the huskiness of her voice, grinding her teeth when she saw the devilish quirk of his brow. Darn him, he knew exactly what his presence was doing to her. "I'll check the phone lines. If they're working, I'll call. In the meantime…" She looked at Emily and Sophie, hoping she did so with aplomb. That peek of thigh beneath his towel was giving her fits. She cleared her throat. "In the meantime, you girls go on into the kitchen. I'll be right in to start breakfast."

Sophie hopped down off the toilet and lost her hold on the cat. It took off in a blur of black and white. Squealing, shoving for position, bickering over who got to go first and the fastest, the girls raced past, hot on its trail, nearly knocking Chelsa over in their rush.

"Here, now. No running in the house!"

Both girls skidded comically to a halt.

"But the kitty's runnin'," Sophie pointed out, her wide blue eyes full of innocence.

"Well, then, it'll have to learn the rules, won't it?"

"We better go tell him," Emily whispered, urging her little sister into a fast tiptoe that was merely a more controlled style of running.

Biting her cheeks to contain her grin, Chelsa shook

her head and watched them go. One minute they were ready to brawl, and the next they were so sweet to one another it nearly brought tears to her eyes.

The smell of shaving cream permeated her senses. When she turned, her shoulder butted into Antonio's chest. Evidently, he, too, had been watching the escapade.

And he was standing entirely too close.

Realization flashed like a blinding neon sign, knocking her shaky control right off its axis. Neither one of them was wearing enough clothes for Chelsa's peace of mind.

Wrapped up in what he was wearing—or *not* wearing, rather—she'd neglected to think about her own state of undress. The T-shirt emblazoned with kissing frogs and hearts was modest enough…for parading in front of her daughters. Certainly not for wearing in the company of a virile stranger.

Flustered, she said the first thing that came to mind. ''Whose razor were you using?''

''Yours, I assume. Alas, I neglected to grab my travel bag when the *Diablo Plata* was making a beeline for the reef.''

''I thought that shaving cream smelled familiar.'' What an inane thing to say. Good night, he was close. Her heart was knocking against her ribs, so loud, she wondered if he could hear it.

''Will your little girls question my masculinity again, do you think?''

She tugged at the hem of her nightshirt, and bit her lip, fighting the smile. ''I—I don't believe that was ever in question.''

His head dipped closer.

Chelsa slapped a palm against his chest, holding

him off. "That's quite an appetite you have there, Prince."

"You do not know the half of it." His smooth Latin accent lowered his voice, turned it intimate. "And ridiculous as it may seem, I am finding that I am quite envious of those two frogs on your night-clothes."

Chelsa's gaze whipped down. Sure enough, each stencil covered her breasts, hugging them, caressing them, creating images of…

Get a grip! She whirled and practically ran out of the bathroom. "Get dressed. We'll be in the kitchen." Hopefully food would satisfy *both* their appetites.

She seriously doubted it.

By doggies, why had her body chosen now of all times to betray her? This behavior wouldn't do at all!

WHEN ANTONIO GOT to the kitchen, Chelsa was frying bacon. She'd donned another of her feminine dresses that skimmed her ankles, and her flyaway hair had been subdued into a ponytail. With its natural curl, it still looked tousled and sexy. He'd always been partial to smooth, sleek hair. Wavy tresses the color of ripe wheat were starting to top his list of erotic sights.

"Did you check the phones?"

She jumped, splattering bacon grease on the floor. "I wish you'd make a little more noise," she complained.

He grinned, pleased that he got to her. Stepping up behind her, he tore off a sheet from the paper towel rack and bent to wipe up the grease. "Moving quietly is an art I acquired as a boy. It was great fun to slip around the hallways of the palace and catch the royal subjects unaware." Straightening, he tossed the towel into the trash and reached past her to rinse his hands. "So, are the phones up and running?"

"I haven't checked." She glanced at the girls who were showering so much attention on that pitiful cat, it was a wonder it had any fur left. "I thought I'd wait until after breakfast."

"No hurry." He ambled over to the table, grinning as Emily shoved a bowl of milk under the cat's nose. "Perhaps he is no longer thirsty," he said, and could have sworn the cat gave him a grateful look.

"But he's skinny," Emily protested.

"Yes, but he'll want to start slow with his eating. Otherwise he might get sick right here in the dining hall. That would be an embarrassing breach of manners for any man."

"How come you call him a man?" Sophie asked.

Antonio discreetly lifted the cat's tail. "Because he is of the male gender, and I would not want to offend by calling him a mere boy."

"See," Emily said, aiming a look at her sister. "I told you, you couldn't name him after you. Besides, Sophie's a dumb name for a kitty."

"Well, he can't be the Emily baby, either," Sophie argued.

"Girls," Chelsa interrupted. "The kitty might already have a name."

"Nuh-uh!"

She placed the bacon on a rack to drain and whipped eggs. "He might have a family who's looking for him," she said gently.

"But he's stayin' wif us," Sophie pointed out, folding her pudgy hands in front of her. "He gots to have a name."

"Why don't we just address him as Kitty for now?" Antonio suggested. "He'll more than likely recognize that title and respond."

Emily patted the cat. "But he's a boy."

Antonio reached down and covered the cat's ears, pretending horror. "Shh. A man, if you please."

Both little girls went into gales of giggles and looked at him with utter adoration. It gave him a punch right in the solar plexus.

"How do you say Mr. Kitty in Spanish?" Emily asked.

"Señor Gatito."

Emily mimicked his accent fairly well. Sophie had a little more trouble getting her tongue around the syllables. A whispered discussion ensued, and Emily coached Sophie in pronunciation. From the hugs and kisses and fur ruffling, it looked as if the cat now had a name in spite of their mother's warning.

"Breakfast," Chelsa announced, just as the phone pealed.

The platter of eggs slipped from her hands and landed in a heap on the floor.

The cat pounced, the girls scrambled after it, shrieking admonishments, and Chelsa still stood frozen in place, staring at the telephone as though it was a loaded gun aimed directly at her heart.

Despite the chaos, Antonio's main concern was the delicate woman who'd become so pale and motionless. Keeping his eyes fixed on her, he lifted the receiver, listened, then replaced the instrument.

Stepping over to Chelsa, he gently cupped her cheek. "It was the repair company, giving a courtesy call to let us know the lines are working."

Her blue eyes appeared dazed.

"Chelsa?" Softly, carefully, he pressed his lips to her forehead. *¡Dios!* He hated to see the terror that paralyzed her.

She blinked. "I've made a mess."

"Señor Gatito and I will take care of it. Sit."

She glanced at the scattered remains of breakfast. "No, I'll need to fix more eggs."

"Sit, *querida*."

She shook her head, apology in her eyes. "I'm sorry. I was just startled for a minute. I'm fine now."

Short of forcing her, there was nothing he could do, and that annoyed him. He was used to getting his way.

Locating the broom and dust pan, he nudged the cat out of the way and swept up the soggy eggs. Thankfully the platter had been plastic, so there was no glass to contend with. As he dealt with the floor, Chelsa cracked more eggs into the skillet. When her hands shook, he refrained from commenting.

It wasn't right, he thought. She was a woman alone, with the responsibility of raising two sweet little girls. She should not have to fear the phone every time it rang.

And what exactly was it that she feared? Oh, he knew about the threat, but he wasn't certain what nightmare scenarios she might be building in that creative mind of hers.

With the floor sponged clean, he moved beside her. "Is there a call in particular you are dreading?" he asked quietly.

She'd gotten herself back under control, he noticed. Her hands were quick and efficient as she scraped the spatula over the coated surface of the skillet. "Mitch said he'd call if there was news of Rick's release."

He knew it was important to be prepared, but he wished she could be spared the knowing. "In the meantime, we are operating under the assumption that he is still in prison?"

"Yes." She scooped fluffy eggs into a clean bowl and he took it from her. She smiled a bit sheepishly. "Don't trust me not to drop the second batch of breakfast?"

He returned the grin. "We would not want Señor Gatito to overindulge."

The worry crept back into her eyes. She laid a hand on his arm before he could move to the table. "I'm not sure it's such a good idea to let the girls name the cat. If the owner's found, they'll have to give him up. Naming him makes it more personal, and it'll be harder on them."

Left unspoken were the other relationships they'd given up. Their father's topping the list.

"I do not think we can prevent them from doing so. If an owner is located, we will simply replace this stray with a new one. One that they may keep unconditionally." He raised a brow in question. "Provided that is acceptable to you, of course."

"I don't mind them having a pet. It's just that...well, the timing isn't great."

Because they were essentially on the run. Fleeing with the girls was one thing. Adding an animal to the mix was another. "I will make you a deal. If at any time you are unable to keep the cat, you may call on me and I will stand in as a pet-sitter."

Chelsa muffled a chuckle at that particular image. "I'm sorry, I can't quite picture stray cats at the palace." Then again, she would never have pictured a prince mopping up her kitchen floor, either.

"Well, there are none to date. However, last I heard, Princess Briana had dragged home a mutt of questionable lineage. From accounts by extremely reliable sources, I understand it is creating all manner of chaos."

"You say that with such glee." Together they set the food on the table.

"Ah, yes." He grinned and held her chair out as though he were a gallant escort treating her at a five-star restaurant. "Anything that shakes up the *palacio* is of great interest to me."

"You're bad." She sat down and tried to control her reaction when his hand brushed her shoulder. Kisses on the forehead, a skimming of fingertips here and there. The man was a toucher by nature. She wondered if every woman reacted as strongly as she did— or if underexercised hormones were to blame.

"Girls, put the cat down and eat. No—" she held up a hand to silence the protests that automatically brewed. "Señor Gatito dined at the first seating. I'm sure he's full now." Good night, she was starting to sound like Antonio. The tiny kitchen could hardly be compared to fine dining accommodations. And darn it all, she'd automatically called that scrawny cat by its adopted name.

"Girls," she said again when they didn't immediately react to her directive.

Grumbling, neither one wanting to relinquish their hold, Emily and Sophie finally managed to set the cat on the floor. Good thing their movements were fairly well synchronized, otherwise the poor cat would have ended up as an unwilling contortionist.

"I have a suggestion," Antonio announced. "Rather than calling the information center, the four of us can go into town and post a notice on the bulletin board. If anyone has lost their pet, that will be the first place they look.''

The girls' expressions vacillated between excitement over getting out of the house, and mutiny over the possibility of having to give up their newly adopted pet.

Aside from her daughters' issues, Chelsa automatically resisted. ''A phone call will accomplish the same thing.''

Antonio, being the astute man he was, noticed her evasion. He reached over and covered her hand with his. ''You need to get out, *querida*. And I need to purchase additional clothes.'' His dark eyes held her, enticed her. ''Come to town with me.'' He brought out the big guns next. ''Sophie and Emily need to feel a sense of normality.''

''That's not fair.'' His reminder stung. ''They aren't lacking in activities. The private beach and the water keeps them plenty busy…and happy.''

''And away from people.''

Her chin jutted forward, her eyes meeting his squarely. ''Yes.''

''I thought we had moved past the trust issue. I would not steer you wrong.''

''Not deliberately. But I think you don't realize your effect on people. You can't control everything and everyone around you.''

''Chelsa, Chelsa.'' He shook his head. ''You have not been paying attention. I grew up around here. Ernesto Vicente taught me to fish when I was barely Sophie's age, and his wife, Alicia, tanned my hide when I attempted to fly from the roof overhang of her fruit stand.''

Astonished, Chelsa laughed. "You didn't."

"I did. The tablecloth was a miscalculation on my part. It did not make an effective parachute." He glanced at the girls who were listening avidly. "You must learn from my mistakes, *niñas,* and never attempt such a folly."

The girls shook their heads.

Chelsa pushed back a stray curl that had escaped her ponytail. "And the woman actually spanked you? A *prince?*"

"Absolutely. And in front of the queen, too, who watched with entirely too much satisfaction, if you ask me." He shook his head, his dimples winking boyishly. "You must believe me, *querida.* To the people of San Alegra, I am merely one of their family. They are not impressed by my money."

"Or your title?"

"I do not use the title," he dismissed. "Come. Let us explore, see if anyone is missing a scrawny cat, shop a bit." He stood and pulled Chelsa to her feet. Sophie and Emily scrambled down from the table, dancing around them, begging for an affirmative answer from Chelsa.

Oh, she was losing ground fast.

"Say yes," he urged, adding an intimacy to his deep voice that was so hot, it nearly singed her.

She couldn't hold out against their pleading. *Imagine,* she thought, *a prince begging.* It tickled her.

Besides, with the storm they'd just had, and the ferry not due for five days yet, it wasn't likely that Rick would show up—provided he was actually out of prison, she reasoned. And if he was, Mitch would have called her.

She'd told the girls this was a vacation. It was time to set aside her fears and not disappoint her daughters.

They'd had too many disappointments as it was.

"All right, you win," she said, earning herself a gentle smile from Antonio and exuberant hugs from Emily and Sophie. Lord, the scene here in the kitchen was like one big happy family.

She was going to have to remember not to buy in to that fantasy.

IT WASN'T A FAR WALK into town. Sophie wasn't thrilled when she'd found out they'd have to leave Señor Gatito at home, but Emily's six-year-old wisdom soon set the frown to rights when she reasoned that nobody else could claim him if he was hiding in the house.

The sandy pathway, shaded by palms and ferns and sweet-smelling orchids soon gave way to more rural terrain as they reached the main road into town. A herd of goats cropped in a grassy field where white farmhouses and windmills dotted the land. All around them, the verdant expanse was carpeted by rich color and scent. Wildflowers flourished even in the cracks of the uneven pavement, pushing their happy faces toward the sun, while Spanish broom with its vibrant yellow blooms dotted the meadows.

It all seemed so tranquil, so innocent and fresh, but with the girls skipping ahead in carefree abandon, chasing butterflies and stray sheep, Chelsa couldn't totally quell her nerves.

Obviously Antonio noticed.

"None of that, *querida.* The sun is shining and the birds are singing. You must think only happy thoughts, enjoy the adventure."

She glanced at him. He wore his leather deck shoes without socks. Although his shirt was wrinkled—and missing a couple of buttons—his jeans had held up nicely through his shipwreck ordeal.

"Do you look at everything as an adventure?"

"Of course. I am dedicated to the art of having fun. In fact, if I am not mistaken, I believe there are some ponies just over the rise there. Mr. Benito frowns on people taking them for joyrides, but I'm betting he would turn a blind eye if the girls sneaked a quick trot around the path."

She laughed despite herself. The man was incorrigible. "Do you work?"

"Play is my work." He grinned at her, his dimples carving deep furrows in his lean cheeks. "Do not look at me like that. I earn excellent money in my pursuits."

"Bragging, Your Highness?"

He tisked at her use of the title. "Merely convincing you that I am not a lazy bum. Tell me, *bella*. Would you tie yourself behind a desk or in a stuffy meeting with dignitaries and trade squabbles if you were making twenty-five-million American dollars on a single Grand Prix race?"

"Good night! That's obscene."

He laughed. "There's another eight million that comes with endorsements."

"How do you even begin to spend that kind of money?"

"Who has time to spend? When I am not working at play, I am working at managing the investments and attending charity functions."

He touched her waist, gallantly steering her away from a thorny bush. "However, I will endeavor to spend some in town. You and the girls may pick out whatever you like. It will be my treat, my way of thanking you for the rescue and hospitality.''

''That isn't necessary. Us Southerners are taught to be gracious. Besides, did your money make it on shore with you?''

''In San Alegra, I do not need bank notes. My credit is excellent.''

Which served as a swift, stark reminder that he was well-known. Not just here, but worldwide. Her heart gave an extra punch to her ribs. ''Emily,'' she called. ''You and Sophie wait for us. You're getting too far ahead.'' She held out her hand, needing to touch them, to hold them close, to make sure they were safe.

''They are within our sight, *querida*. Nothing will harm them.''

She ignored his gentle admonishment. She might appear overprotective to him, but that was the way things were.

''You can count on me, Chelsa. Except...'' He seemed to wrestle with himself over his next words.

''Except what?''

The hesitation was slight. ''Do not trust me with your heart. I would not hurt you for the world.''

''No danger there. My heart has a thick wall around it.'' She glanced away so he wouldn't see the lie. She was terribly afraid that the wall was crumbling. But that wasn't his problem. He was honest in his intentions.

And honesty was something she valued highly. Respected.

She felt much better once Emily and Sophie slipped their hands into hers. It gave her pause, though, when

Emily turned flirty eyes up to Antonio and reached for his hand also.

One big happy family, she thought again, and tried to dismiss the image from her mind. She'd been warned, gently to be sure, and with sincere compassion. It wasn't Antonio's fault that he was a man who inspired feminine fantasies, a man who made a woman automatically hope and dream and wish.

She set aside those impossible thoughts as they rounded the corner into the center of town that was quaint and welcoming. She'd been there before, to get supplies when she'd arrived. She hadn't lingered, though; her nerves had been too tied in knots to appreciate the beauty.

And although the edges of fear would never truly be banished until there was some sort of closure with Rick, Antonio's solid presence and good-faith promises somehow allowed her to contain it to a manageable level, allowed her to at least appreciate the beauty of her surroundings.

Floral arches spanned the narrow streets, connecting the vine-covered buildings. Boutiques, bars and restaurants lined the *Calle de las Flores*—street of the flowers. The air smelled sweet, of violets and lavender.

Farther down the street were buildings with façades painted in pastels and balconies draped with flowerpots. A sidewalk restaurant with white plastic tables and chairs and bright umbrellas invited customers to relax and enjoy the unhurried ambiance.

The cake shop they passed, with its impressive display of chocolate sculptures and confectionary, caused the girls to go into a near trance. Chelsa urged them forward, earning herself a hound-dog look from her three companions. Well, honestly, she thought. The wonderful smell alone would add three inches to her thighs.

"We will sneak back when she's not looking," Antonio assured the girls in a stage whisper. "But first we must shop, and I have a very special place in mind."

"Do we have to ask the people about Señor Gatito?" Emily asked.

"Yes, little one. It would only be fair. You would not want another family to be sad over the loss of their pet, would you?"

Emily shook her head. Sophie just looked at him, obviously considering the merits of omission.

Antonio grinned. "Come. My friends will know if Señor Gatito is missing from a home. They know everyone on the island and the animals, too."

"Can you buy me candy?" Sophie asked.

Chelsa opened her mouth to scold. Emily beat her to the punch. "It's not nice to ask people for stuff, Sophie." Cunningly she lifted inquisitive blue eyes to Antonio, feigning proper manners when it was more than obvious that she'd like to hear his answer.

He laughed. "But I have already promised to lead a shopping spree. If candy is on the wish list, then we will clean out the store."

"I don't think—"

Before Chelsa could finish, he placed a finger over her lips. "You must not spoil my fun, now. I am wanting to repay the three of you for rescuing me." When she automatically started to argue, he hit her with the one thing she couldn't refute. "And my friends operate their store on very little profit. Whether I need items or not, I make it a point to purchase many things so their till will ring favorably at the end of the week.''

''You come here that often?''

''At least once a month. Alicia and Ernesto are treasured friends.''

And very lucky to have the genuine devotion of someone like Antonio Castillo. Admiration sent a host of giddy butterflies loose in her stomach and she relented with good grace. He was like a happiness fairy, generously spreading goodwill wherever he went while leaving a person's pride intact.

''In that case,'' she said. ''Lead on. I've always wanted to watch someone else hurt their credit card. I imagine you can manage that like a pro.''

''A pro, yes. But I assure you, *querida,* my credit cards are so fat, there is no way to hurt them.''

She gave him a playful shove, amazed at the sparks that zinged up her arm at the contact. ''Bragger.''

''Ah, no, *bella.*'' His gaze, when it focused solely on her, was exquisitely, breathtakingly intimate. As was the thumb he swept gently over her bottom lip. ''I do not need to brag.''

Chelsa wondered if they'd somehow changed altitudes on their trek into town. Suddenly she was unable to draw a decent breath. It didn't take a rocket scientist to figure out he wasn't talking about money.

He was referring to sex—a subject that was starting to take center stage in every one of her waking and sleeping thoughts.

Chapter Six

Chelsa was sure everyone in the small store would notice her flushed cheeks and breathlessness, but that wasn't the case. The tiny woman who came charging around the counter had eyes only for Antonio.

Exclaiming, chattering rapidly in Spanish, she kissed him on both cheeks and inspected him like a mother hen who'd just found her missing chick. She clucked over the bruise on his head and tisked at the missing buttons on his shirt, her brows drawn in worry.

Antonio allowed her to fawn, and Chelsa marveled at the sight. The woman was by no means royalty; her modest clothing and unpretentious style silently testified to her humble roots. Yet he treated her with the deference due a queen.

And rightly so, Chelsa thought with an inward giggle. This woman had paddled his behind! It was an image she couldn't quite get to gel.

At last noticing Chelsa and the girls, Alicia turned, giving Antonio a smart pinch on the arm for leaving guests standing about.

"Come," she said to Chelsa in English. "The boy has no manners and makes me forget my own. Ernesto!'' she shouted over her shoulder. ''We have guests.''

''You wound me, maligning my character, Señora Vicente,'' Antonio said in mock affront. ''I would have performed introductions immediately had you not snatched me straight to your bosom.''

''Oh, you are an impertinent scoundrel. Introduce me to your companions.''

He grinned and extended a hand to Ernesto who'd just wandered out of the back room at his wife's summons.

''Alicia and Ernesto Vicente, I'd like you to meet my rescuers, Chelsa Lawrence and her daughters, Emily and Sophie. If not for them, I would be shark bait.''

''He exaggerates,'' Chelsa said, moving forward, her hand extended. Ignoring the traditional Western greeting, Alicia pulled her into an embrace and kissed both cheeks, then treated the girls to the same. Sophie and Emily lit up like fireflies on a hot summer night. It had been a while since they'd been on the receiving end of such grandmotherly attention.

And Chelsa decided right then and there that what Antonio had said was true. These people would guard their own with a fierceness that was unquestionable.

''He always exaggerates,'' Alicia said. ''But I think in this case he speaks the truth, and for that you have our deepest gratitude. This boy is like a son to us, and I have the white hairs to prove it.'' She sent Antonio an arch look.

''He told me about trying to fly off the roof,'' Chelsa said.

Alicia shook her head. ''That was tame compared to some of his other stunts. But if I listed his misdeeds we would be here all day, and I would have stomach pains in remembering.'' She straightened a display of seashells. ''Now then, Antonio usually makes frivolous purchases, although he does not know that I realize what he is doing.'' She cast a loving eye his way, then looked back at Chelsa. ''You, however, must not strain your budget. It is expensive these days to raise children, so I make you a good deal on whatever you need.''

''I don't really—''

''I am in need of clothing,'' Antonio interrupted. ''And the girls must have candy, and for Chelsa, something pretty and fun and impulsive is in order.'' The look he sent her caused her toes to curl. He was so sure of himself. And so thrilling.

''You're awfully bossy.'' She couldn't muster any sternness to give her words punch.

Alicia laughed. ''He thinks everyone should share his ideas. And, to an extent, I think we all do.'' Like a tiny dictator, she pointed and waved and issued orders, proving that she was indeed worthy of giving Antonio a run for his money. ''Pick out your clothes, Antonio. There are no fussy maids to do your bidding, and you know where the merchandise is. Ernesto, you take these precious *niñas* and fill their sacks with sweets. And you, *bonita*,'' she said, linking her arm with Chelsa's, ''I will keep entertained. No one comes to Vicente's and is pressured to buy.''

''I have money—''

''No, no. We will talk.''

Chelsa stifled a grin. She imagined Alicia was going to talk and she was going to listen. That was okay. In learning to guard her privacy, she sometimes wondered if she'd lost her conversational skills. Around these people, it didn't appear to matter. They interrupted at will.

"So, you rescued our boy. And you like him, no?"

"Well—"

"You be careful around that one. He is slippery."

Chelsa glanced at Antonio—even the lure of candy hadn't kept the girls from flocking to him. They giggled at something he said, added their opinions to his clothing choices and danced around him like gamboling puppies.

The sight and sound of their happiness—a happiness brought about by a playboy prince—caused her eyes to sting and her stomach to flutter. Especially when he looked up and caught her staring, giving her a smile that wrapped around her heart and squeezed.

Alicia noticed the warm look and nodded. *"Bueno,"* she said softly.

Chelsa frowned, flustered, and attempted to nip any assumptions before they bloomed. "He's only a friend, Mrs. Vicente—"

"Alicia."

"Of course. Alicia, I'm here on holiday with my daughters. Antonio is only staying because his yacht was wrecked, and as soon as the ferry comes, he'll be leaving."

"I have cautioned you to be careful, but I am wondering.… I have a hobby," she said, causing Chelsa to scramble in order to keep up with the subject. "I study names and see if they fit the person. It is a rule in my family that expectant women must consult me before naming their offspring."

Chelsa wasn't sure if she was about to be reprimanded or praised for her own choices. "Dare I admit that I never looked up the meanings of my children's names?''

''Most people do not. But you have chosen well. Emily means 'flatterer,' and one only has to look to see that she is good at that.''

Chelsa grinned. ''Yes. She can wrap me around her little finger before I even realize what she's doing.''

Alicia nodded. ''And Sophie is 'wisdom.' The child is imitating her sister's excitement, but there is a solemnness to her. Her little mind is churning with thought.''

Astonished by the insight, Chelsa watched her daughters. ''You have keen senses to identify their traits so accurately by just looking at them.''

''And you, Chelsa, are a port of ships.''

''No—''

''Yes, and I believe you are exactly what our wanderlust sailor needs.''

For no good reason, her heart fluttered against her ribs. ''I told you, we're just friends. Once the ferry comes, he'll be gone.''

Alicia gave a gentle, speculative smile. ''There is no need for him to wait for the ferry, *bonita*. Ernesto could deliver Antonio to the mainland in his fishing boat at any time.''

Stunned, Chelsa stood there mute, grappling with this new piece of information. When another customer entered the store, Alicia started to turn away, then hesitated.

''And Antonio means 'priceless.' The woman who represents the special harbor he is searching for will indeed be getting a priceless treasure—a gem that the fancy people of the world do not realize exists. And that gem, to that special port of wanderlust ships, is priceless indeed.''

As she watched Alicia greet her newest customer with the customary kiss on both cheeks, Chelsa concentrated on bringing her heart rate under control. No matter what the woman said, Antonio wasn't looking for a port of ships to settle down with, and Chelsa wasn't looking for a gem, priceless or otherwise.

Besides, she didn't place that much importance on the meaning of a name. They were just names.

And she did not, under any circumstances, want hers linked to Antonio Castillo's. That would be like attaching a homing device to herself, giving Rick the advantage of keeping tabs on her for the rest of her life.

And that was dangerous.

She wanted her life to be a long one. She wanted to see her children grow up, watch them graduate from high school, from college, watch them fall in love and have families of their own.

And to ensure that that happened, she'd do anything, sacrifice anything. And she would not—could not—let herself entertain fantasies about ports for wayward ships and dreamy princes seeking mooring.

''You are deep in thought, *querida*.''

Antonio's soft words gave her a jolt and she nearly screamed. ''You scared the devil out of me!''

''I apologize. But you were looking a little lost and down, and I felt it my utmost duty to remind you we are on an adventure to have fun.''

His teasing put things back in perspective. This wasn't a man looking for a permanent berth to dock his ship. And on the subject of ships...

''Alicia mentioned that you're not actually stranded

as I thought. Evidently Ernesto can ferry you home anytime you like?''

''Did I lead you to believe I was stranded?''

''Yes.''

''Must have been the knock on my head.''

''Try again, Prince.''

''Tony,'' he coached. He sighed when she didn't budge. ''To be honest, in the beginning it did not occur to me to seek out Ernesto. Perhaps because I was intrigued—or blinded rather—by your beauty.'' He reached for her hand. ''No, do not go all stiff and bristly on me. I am speaking from my heart with genuine honesty.''

She relaxed. The one thing she was sure she could count on was his honesty. ''So why are you here buying enough clothes to last you the week, then? Why aren't you sailing back home where you probably have room-size closets filled with outfits?''

''Like I said, it crossed my mind to stay and get to know you…for myself. Now I would like to stay for you. You rescued me, *querida*. I would like to be around in the event that you, too, might need rescuing.''

Just the words raised eerie chills along her arms, made nausea churn in her stomach. ''We'll be fine.''

''I am sure that is so. But I am a man who likes to see and do things for himself. A bit of a control freak, if you must know. If I left the island, I would worry. And not knowing if matters had been resolved between the authorities and Rick—and you—would eat me alive. So you see, you are in turn doing me another favor. You are saving my sanity.''

''I thought we'd already established that your sanity was nonexistent in the first place.''

For once he ignored her pitiful attempt at humor.

"You must not split hairs, *querida*. If you insist, I will take a room at the hotel, but I would much rather that you agree to allow me the use of your porch. There is nothing pressing for me to get back to at home. I have time on my hands, and I would like to see you through your dilemma—or at least see you to safety."

Oh, it was so tempting. To know there was an ally. To know she wasn't alone. But dragging someone else into her private hell...? And a prince at that.

He bent his knees, bringing his face even with hers. "I will be like a guard dog, lying across your threshold."

The image was so crazy, she burst out laughing, drawing the attention of the Vicentes who were doing their utmost to spoil Emily and Sophie. "Now you're really getting deep."

"But am I convincing you?"

"I'm thinking about it."

"Shall we ask the opinion of Emily and Sophie?"

"That's not fair."

"Ah, I said you could count on me. I do not recall promising to use fair means in order to get my way."

"No wonder everywhere you go people fall for you. It's that little-boy look with just the right amount of sex appeal that no one can resist."

"You think I'm sexy?" His grin was suggestive enough to make her knees wobble.

"Don't get too confident, Prince. You might be able to sweet-talk my daughters, but I'm a little more discriminating."

"The question is, are you discriminating enough to let me stay on your porch?"

She blew out a resigned breath, knowing when she was outmatched. And secretly pleased in the bargain. ''It's either that, or I'll have a mutiny on my hands and be forced to let the kids move to town with you. My daughters are half in love with you.''

''And I with them.''

Teasing aside, she sobered. ''It'll be hard on them when you leave, Antonio. Be conscious of that.''

''Like I said, I would not hurt you for the world. And that includes your children, too.''

She sincerely hoped that was the case.

''Come,'' he said. ''Now that we have lodging matters settled, you must browse and choose something frivolous. A memento of your stay in San Alegra. My treat, of course.''

She imagined that Antonio would be enough of a memento to last her a lifetime, but she kept that to herself and let him lead her through the store.

There were seashells and jewelry and gaily colored island clothing. In refrigerator boxes, fresh fish— caught by Ernesto—tempted shoppers to plan a meal or a fish fry on the beach over an open campfire.

But it was the framed art on the walls that caught Chelsa's eye.

''Oh, this is beautiful.'' Her hushed voice reflected a sense of awe as she ran her finger over the glass-enclosed photo of a naked baby in a plastic wading pool, flower blossoms floating around her. The baby's head was wreathed with a crown of pink rose buds, and tiny feather wings rested atop her shoulders. So sweet, Chelsa thought. So precious. A closer look showed distinctive, unique eyes set close together, staring out at the world with nothing but love...a Down's syndrome baby.

The name of the photo was *Hope*.

Warmth poured into Chelsa's heart. That single word, as well as the obvious specialness of the baby, were a perfect reminder that there were bigger problems in the world, an invitation to take stock of the many blessings one might be tempted to take for granted.

And the message was cleverly and simply conveyed through the innocence of a child.

"Yes, she is beautiful," Antonio said, his voice just as quiet. "The artist who took this photo comes from a very prominent family in my country. Remember Cole Martinez whom your detective spoke about?"

"Yes."

"Raquel Santiago Martinez is his wife and a very good friend of mine. In fact, she nearly became my sister-in-law."

Chelsa took a discreet look at the price tag. The strong desire to have this print took her by surprise. She didn't normally covet material things with such intensity.

"No need to look for the cost. If it touches you, it will be my gift to you."

She started to object, albeit weakly. She really did want this picture.

"Besides," he said, "all the proceeds from the sale of this art go toward the Down's syndrome Foundation."

"So it would be a write-off for you, a charity contribution."

"No. It would simply be my gift to you."

Any way he put it, she knew she would relent. And

she'd been taught to do so graciously. "Thank you, Tony. I'd love to have this picture."

As they moved to the counter to pay for their purchases, Chelsa noticed Emily and Sophie huddled together in whispered conversation as Alicia Vicente waited patiently for them to come to some sort of decision over their powwow. It gave Chelsa a start to realize she'd let down her protective guard and entrusted her daughters to Alicia and Ernesto's watchful eye.

Holding Sophie's pudgy hand in her own small one, Emily looked up at Alicia, reminding Chelsa of a tiny Southern debutante about to extend a gracious invitation to tea. The only thing that spoiled the image was the twin frowns that marred the girls' brows.

"Momma said we have to ask about Señor Gatito. He's a very pretty kitty that we found on the beach, and we get to keep him if he doesn't already have a home."

Alicia focused her attention on the two solemn girls as though they were discussing important world events. "You have found a kitty? What does he look like?"

"He's black-and-white and he has a hurt on his ear that flops."

"But he didn't bleed," Sophie added, as though that were a necessary addition to the description. "And we could keep him."

"Only if it won't make some other little girl sad," Emily admonished her sister, who in turn gave a mutinous look that indicated she didn't really care who was sad, so long as Señor Gatito could stay.

Alicia smiled. "I believe I know just the kitty you are speaking of. That old tomcat has been known to beg from everyone, yet I do not believe he has family. But we will post a bulletin just in case. Do not worry, *niñas.* I am thinking your Señor Gatito is a lucky cat and that he has at last found himself a good home.''

The girls were overjoyed and Chelsa bent to hug them, letting them know she was proud that they'd taken the responsibility to ask, even though it had been hard for them.

Too bad their pretty behavior didn't last for long.

While Alicia Vicente rang up the purchases and pronounced them worthy, Sophie inspected the photo and dubbed it a very special water baby, claiming she was sure it had been the Sophie baby in Chelsa's series that had kissed this child and made it so beautiful.

That, of course sparked a brief argument—instigated by Emily—over which water baby had done the magical kissing, because Emily was just certain that her namesake character had more appeal.

Although Chelsa was scandalized by her daughters' bickering in public, Alicia was smugly entertained, and aimed a knowing look directly at Chelsa.

''You see, *bonita,* it is as I said. Sophie is wisdom and Emily is flattery. You think about the rest.''

Ignoring Antonio's obvious curiosity, Chelsa nodded dutifully. But she was *not* going to dwell on scenarios where a certain rogue prince moored his wanderlust yacht in her berth. Never mind the sexual undertones of that image, the philosophical ones wouldn't be considered, either.

By the time they left the store, Chelsa was beginning to think they'd need a wagon to transport their purchases. The girls were in candy and trinket heaven, but Antonio apparently wasn't through threatening the health of their teeth.

As promised, and with much giggling and stage whispers, he whisked them into the cake shop and bought enough chocolate to keep the girls bouncing off the walls and on a sugar high for months. Not to mention the pounds and inches that would no doubt settle right on Chelsa's hips.

Halfway back to the bungalow, Chelsa was still shaking her head. Sophie had a chocolate ring around her mouth and a hand-size smear down the front of her dress. Emily wasn't in much better shape, and the bakery bag had suffered a rip during the scuffle over who got to carry it.

"We will put it away and regulate how much they eat at a sitting," Antonio said as a compromise to her concerns.

"Never mind the kids. *I'm* the one we need to worry about hiding it from."

He grinned, glancing down at her. When their eyes met, it was like an explosion of fireworks, blindingly mesmerizing. With a gentle finger, he captured a strand of hair that blew across her mouth and tucked it behind her ear.

Her steps faltered, and suddenly, the act of putting one foot in front of the other became a near impossibility.

Something was happening between them that she felt ill equipped to deal with. The air became charged and expectant. He leaned in close, his breath warm where it brushed her lips. So close. Yet not touching.

"I have a philosophy that one can never have too much candy."

Or sex.

He didn't say it, but he might as well have. His voice was low and intimate and suggestive, and her body responded like a teenager's caught in the grip of untapped hormones. Her gaze settled on his sculpted mouth, and the yearning that swept her was all encompassing. Even the birdsong seemed to take on a sensual cadence. The meadowlark sitting on the telephone wire seemed to be saying *"Do it! Do it! Do it!"*

Good night, she was pathetic. And she needed to get her mind off the subject and somewhere safer.

"So…" She stopped, cleared her throat and ordered her feet to move. "The photographer, Raquel Martinez, you say she was almost your sister-in-law?"

He fell back into step beside her, acting as though the charged moment had never even happened. "Yes. She was betrothed to Joseph from birth."

If he could appear unaffected by their closeness, so could she. "And what happened?"

"Joseph wanted love over duty, and Raquel wanted freedom and a chance to be a bit of a bohemian rather than a proper heiress."

"Couldn't they discuss these desires and come to terms?" *Desire* was a poor choice of words, threatening to send her off on another tangent. She resisted the train of thought. Especially because Antonio seemed to get so much joy over relating the story of his family and friends.

"Rocky was scared to death to make a peep in Joseph's presence, and Joseph, in turn, neglected to even look at her."

Chelsa frowned.

"I know what it sounds like, but the image you are

no doubt picturing is far removed from each of their personalities. You see, Joseph takes his duty very seriously, but he had begun to get bored.... No, *bored* isn't the right word. He was questioning his life. When he turned thirty, he was to become officially, publicly engaged to Raquel, and a marriage was to take place within months. But alas, he skipped out on the ceremony and sailed a yacht to the French Riviera instead.''

"I imagine that shook up the palace."

"You do not know the half of it. I, myself, had missed the betrothal ceremony, and for that hapless breach, the queen was not pleased. She sent me to reason with my brother—which if you truly think about it, makes not a bit of sense. Imagine, me talking someone into marriage.'' His tone and his expression were alight with feigned horror.

"As it turned out, Joseph most definitely had his mind set on marriage,'' he continued, "but not to Raquel. He met Briana Duvaulle in Monte Carlo and fell like a ton of platinum.''

"Oh. How did Raquel feel about that?''

"Pleased as punch. In fact, when Briana refused Joseph's marriage plea, and Joseph had almost resigned himself to upholding duty and marrying the heiress, Raquel shocked the country by fleeing at the last hour.''

"She left a royal prince standing at the altar?'' And here she'd worried over the etiquette of making one sleep on the porch. Suddenly she didn't feel quite so out of step.

"Gutsy, don't you think?'' He laughed. "However, she rendezvoused with the queen, and the two of them pressed upon Briana that she must set aside any foolishness of thinking that a girl from Ohio could not marry a royal prince. So, expecting Raquel to walk down the isle, Joseph nearly blew the whole thing by trying to back out at the last minute.''

Sophie and Emily had abandoned their chocolate and were caught up in the story by now, nearly tripping themselves as they looked up at Antonio instead of watching where they were going.

''But it was Princess Briana who showed up?'' Emily asked dreamily.

''Absolutely. A real-life fairy tale.''

''And she kissed him so he wasn't a sad frog,'' Sophie inserted.

''That she did.''

''And what happened to Raquel?'' Chelsa asked.

''Yeah,'' Emily said. ''And how come you called her Rocky?''

''I call her Rocky because we are very good friends. Actually, she used to liken herself to Rapunzel.'' He ruffled Sophie's cap of short frizzy curls. ''Remember the heiress I told you about who started a chic trend by leaving her long tresses on the floor of a French salon?''

Sophie nodded. Her cupid bow lips rimmed in chocolate were pursed solemnly, causing her pudgy cheeks to puff out.

''Well, Raquel had beautiful, flowing hair past her waist—''

''But you said it was fuzzy.''

''Yes.'' He backtracked smoothly. ''She had beautiful, *fuzzy* hair past her waist, and in her first act of freedom, she had it all cut off.''

''And it was still beautiful?''

''Even more so. And next, she went to a small

village close to Nice, and became a photo artist, taking pictures of babies.''

"Like the water baby you buyed Momma?"

"That was one of them, yes. And Raquel was a happy heiress now that she didn't have to be a princess—"

"She didn't want to be?" Emily's tone was full of disbelief.

"Well, no…"

"Is Joseph mean?"

Ah, hell, Antonio thought. The story was getting out of hand. He'd forgotten about these little girls and their questions. "No, he's not mean. He's very nice, actually. But she did not love him."

"'Cuz he was still a frog, then," Sophie inserted wisely.

"You are very right, little mermaid. I am certain that was the case. So, anyway, Raquel was happy photographing her babies and dressing like a siren—"

"What's a siren?"

He glanced at Chelsa for this one. He wasn't too sure how deeply she'd like him to delve into this particular subject with a four- and six-year-old. She gave him a saucy grin that told him he was on his own. He was actually astonished that she did so. That she was letting him lead the way with the girls was saying something. Before, she'd kept a tight rein, seemed to even resent it when her daughters turned to him.

It was a small victory, one he imagined she didn't even realize she'd conceded, but he'd take it nonetheless.

"You will pay," he murmured for Chelsa's ears alone. To the girls still staring up at him, he said, "A siren is like a mermaid.'' He left out the temptress of men part.

''So she dressed wif a tail?''

Chelsa choked on laughter. ''Need some help, Prince?''

He gave her a narrowed look and told himself it was the heat that made him sweat. ''No thank you. The day I cannot converse with a female is the day they put me in the ground.''

''I offered.''

''And I expressed gratitude. Now,'' he said, focusing his attention on the four-year-old who saw things entirely too literally. ''Raquel did not actually wear a tail like a mermaid. However, she wore her clothing tight—like the tail on a mermaid is tight—and allowed her middle to be exposed. Is that not an accurate description of a mermaid?'' Hopefully he'd deterred them from the siren part.

''Sort of. 'Cept they gots to wear a bra. And da boobies poof out.'' Sophie made a cupping gesture near her own flat chest.

Antonio held his breath to keep from laughing, and glanced at Chelsa to see how she was taking her daughter's pantomime.

The problem was, his intentions short-circuited somewhere along the way, and damn, if his gaze didn't automatically zero in right on her nicely rounded breasts. He hadn't meant to look precisely there, but his eyes operated seemingly of their own volition.

When he finally got control of his unruly eye muscles and met her gaze, he noticed that rather than being scandalized, her blue eyes were brimming with amusement.

Unable to hold it in a second longer, they both sputtered in laughter. Like a couple of fools, they bent double, holding on to each other for support, which in turn prompted Emily and Sophie to join in—even though they weren't sure what was so funny.

Chelsa leaned against Antonio, her sides aching. She couldn't remember the last time she'd laughed so hard, or felt so good. He supported her with an arm around her waist, accepting her weight, as well as the weight of Emily and Sophie who were each collapsed against his thighs and hanging on like monkeys.

With her head resting against his shoulder, she allowed herself a carefree moment to just feel. The gentle breeze was warm and sweet, smelling of flowers and the ocean. She wanted to capture the tranquillity of the moment and put it in a time capsule where it could never be tarnished by worldly intrusions.

His palm cupped her cheek, his fingers delving into her hair. It was a timeless gesture, one that encouraged another person to lean on them, to relax and enjoy.

And Chelsa realized she had no business taking advantage of the moment, or feeling so giddy over the easiness between the four of them.

Especially since they were standing out in the open. Easy, highly visible targets for a camera lens.

Or the scope of a rifle.

She straightened with a jerk and stepped away. He let her go, giving her a quiet look that spoke volumes, a look that said he was sad the fun was over, and that he knew where her thoughts had gone.

Then his enticing grin flashed and his dimples winked.

"Race you to the house," he called and took off

with the children squealing in glee and hot on his heels. Still not totally willing to let her kids out of her sight, Chelsa joined in the chase, though she kept a respectable distance.

She was getting entirely too close to Antonio Castillo as it was.

By the time she caught up with them, Antonio had commandeered the garden hose and was engaged in a rowdy game of duck and run with her daughters. It was so easy, so *natural* for him to play.

She reached in her pocket for the house key, then kicked off her sandals and pulled open the screen door. Sand gritted beneath her feet as she traversed the expanse of wood flooring on the enclosed porch. She frowned, remembering that she'd swept the floor just that morning.

Even before she had the key all the way inserted in the front door lock, she knew something was wrong.

The hairs on her arm stood on end as the knob turned without the aid of the key.

She was fanatical about locking the doors—at least she'd become that way lately.

Sweat dampened her palms and her heart raced so hard, she felt faint. The urge to run nearly overpowered her, yet indecision held her paralyzed. Dear God, what should she do? If she called out, Antonio would come in a second, racing like the cavalry. But, then, so would the girls.

Oh, Lord. She had to be brave, and she felt like the biggest coward.

Fingers trembling like mad, she pulled the key back out of the lock and palmed it, allowing the serrated edge to protrude through her fingers. As a weapon, it was a pitiful one, but better than nothing.

Leaning against the door, she carefully, with excruciating slowness, turned the knob....

And screamed when a hand clamped on her shoulder.

Chapter Seven

Antonio snatched his hand back so fast, he nearly lost his balance. He wasn't used to women screaming in holy terror when he touched them.

"Easy, *querida*," he soothed. Taking her gently by the shoulders, he turned her to face him. When he got a good look at her, his fighting instincts went on full alert. Her face was pale, her freckles standing out against her milky complexion. It was eighty degrees out, yet goose bumps dotted her skin. Her eyes were wide and liquid, the pupils dilated, and even still he could see her grappling for strength. *¡Dios!* It made him ache to see her torment. "What is it?"

"The door... I locked it..."

He glanced at the door standing slightly ajar, then at the key sticking out from between her fingers. His face went taut when he realized she'd felt the need to arm herself. Inadequately, to be sure, but armed nonetheless. "Go outside with the girls."

"Momma?" Emily said, her voice wobbling. "Why did you scream?"

"I'm sorry, honey—"

"It is very possible a nasty snake slithered past the doorway," Antonio said, saving her an explanation that would only frighten the children more. And the snake description wasn't too far of a fabrication. If Chelsa's ex was on the loose, he was indeed a venomous asp. "If you three *bellas* would kindly wait outdoors, I will endeavor to conduct a search-and-destroy mission."

"Tony, no. That's my responsibility."

He pressed a finger to her lips. "Trust me, *querida*."

Chelsa didn't have much choice. She didn't want Emily and Sophie caught in the cross fire of confrontation if there was an intruder in the house.

She nodded and herded the kids back onto the beach, wrapping her arms around them. They clung, sensing there was more going on than the adults were telling, but they didn't press.

It was sad that they'd been conditioned to silence their fears at such a young age. Chelsa had tried not to lie to them about Rick, but then she'd also tried to downplay the danger. After all, there was a chance that Rick wouldn't follow through on his threat.

A slim one, but a chance nonetheless.

It seemed to take forever before Antonio appeared back on the porch. By then, Chelsa had created all kinds of horrible scenarios. Dear Lord, if she was the cause of harm to this celebrated prince, she would never forgive herself. Nor would his countrymen of Valldoria, she suspected.

But her nightmare images were put to rest by his winning grin. The light expression was for Emily and Sophie's benefit, she suspected. And maybe for her own. But she looked past the carefree flash of dimple and perfect white teeth to his dark eyes.

They were worried.

Her heart kicked into another runaway gallop and her arms tightened around her children.

"All clear," he announced.

"Did you find the snake?" Emily asked.

"Did it have big teeth?" Sophie's eyes were round and inquisitive. Emily shot her sister an annoyed look.

"No uninvited animals in the house. Señor Gatito did an excellent job of guarding the fortress while we were away."

The girls broke loose of Chelsa's hold and raced into the house. Evidently they'd forgotten about their newly acquired pet.

Chelsa followed more slowly, needing to look for herself. She still felt disturbed, as though unseen eyes were trained on her. She shivered, then went still as a pillar of salt.

Resting on the closed lid of her laptop computer was a shiny, 1992 quarter—tails up.

1992…the year she'd married Rick Lawrence.

The buzzing in her ears was like a chorus of locusts in mating season. She couldn't hear. She couldn't think. Perspiration beaded on her upper lip, trickled between her breasts, slicked her fingers. She didn't reach for the coin.

She glanced at Antonio. "You checked the whole house?" It was as though her words were a mere echo in her head, ricocheting off an invisible wall, then sucked into a vacuum. "The closets? Under the beds?"

"Yes." He came up beside her, searched her face. "Everywhere."

The girls were within sight, showering attention on the cat. If need be, she could reach them within seconds. "He's been here," she whispered.

"Chelsa—"

"Look." She pointed to the computer. "Rick loved money, loved the feel of change. He was always tossing me a penny—for luck, he'd say. That was when he was in a good mood. When he was unhappy with me or life or the brand of the cereal, or if he just wanted to get my attention, he'd leave a single quarter, tails up, where he knew I'd find it."

"And the significance?"

She shrugged. "It was his slimy way of saying that whatever or whoever upset him wasn't worth two bits."

The meaning this time was clear. Her life wasn't worth two bits.

And Rick was cunning. He had the type of mind that could plot an "accident" and probably get away with it. Oh, she could see it now. The grieving ex—sorry for his past mistakes—convincing a system he'd gone straight and learned his lesson. He'd be able to pull off such an act. And under Mississippi law, he could gain legal guardianship of their daughters if she were dead.

Not that he wanted anything to do with the girls. He only wanted to make Chelsa pay.

With her life.

How could she have been so wrong about the man she'd married? Starry-eyed and young, she'd had such hopes. She'd never *seen* Rick resort to physical violence, but she'd seen his desperation there at the end, a madness that told her he'd crossed the line. And she'd heard it in his voice, too.

Anything was possible…even probable.

She turned suddenly, feeling as though the ground beneath her was unpredictable quicksand. "Promise me something, Tony.'' Her voice was a low, fierce whisper. ''If anything happens to me, take care of my girls.''

''Shh, nothing will—''

''Promise me,'' she begged, making a conscious effort not to scream. Tears welled and no amount of fighting could call them back. ''Make sure they're cared for. You have connections.'' She gripped the front of his shirt, ripping off another of his buttons. The plastic disk bounced off the hardwood floor like a shot and rolled to a stop onto the braided rug. ''Promise me.''

Antonio snatched her to him and held on. ''I promise.'' The vow was sealed before he'd even given the ramifications a second thought.

¡Madre de Dios! What had he done? He'd never gone back on a promise, never made ones that he couldn't keep. Yet he'd just vowed to uphold an enormous responsibility.

Nothing was going to happen to her, he thought fiercely. He'd see to it. But how? He couldn't buy his way—or hers—out of this danger.

The only thing he could do was stick around and use his brawn and wits to protect her. Because now, especially now, the thought of leaving her alone was intolerable.

A queer sensation raced through his body. She was a beautiful woman. Her daughters were angels. But he was not a man to settle down to hearth and home. This funny feeling in his chest did *not* mean he was falling for her.

He was simply giving comfort, being a friend. Yet as he held her slight body, he felt his own respond. And the sensation was anything but friendship.

Since there were children in the room—although the cat captured their sole attention—he eased back, reaching deep for a measure of control.

Chelsa had obviously found her own well of strength, because her face was no longer pale. In fact, her cheeks were blushed with color. At any other time, under any other circumstances, he would have taken advantage of the obvious arousal.

But Chelsa was different. She was special. With her, his usual, easy charm didn't seem appropriate—his the-world-is-my-oyster attitude no longer seemed appropriate.

"What about your family, *querida?*"

"What about them?"

"You must have parents. Sophie speaks of a grandpa who removes his teeth—they resemble snapping alligators, she says."

Chelsa smiled. Just being held, knowing that someone else was here to lean on occasionally, was enough to restore her equilibrium. "That would be my dad."

"You are in San Alegra. Could you not go to him?"

"Yes. But it was my choice not to. I don't want anyone else dragged into danger—if there is any." The tacked-on statement was a last-ditch hold on rationality, on the odds. But she wasn't one to play the odds, and a sixth sense told her she wasn't overreacting. She released a breath.

"However, it looks as though I've inadvertently dragged you into the mess. You'd be smart to pack up your new clothes and hit up Ernesto for a ride home."

"You haven't dragged me anywhere I do not want to go." He traced a finger down her cheek. "It is like

I said. You ask nothing of others, and instead take it all on your shoulders. But that is no longer necessary, because I'm staying.''

His words both thrilled and worried her. He did make her feel safe, though…or at least safer. And short of throwing him out bodily, she didn't think she could change his mind, or budge him. So she nodded. ''Thank you.''

''Do you have a gun?''

Her eyes widened as the implications of a new and horrible thought crowded in. ''Yes. Mitch insisted. I put it up in the top of the closet—I didn't want the kids to find it.'' She swept past him, and raced to the bedroom. She reached for the sliding wardrobe door, then hesitated. What if it was missing? What if there was something more than clothes in the dark alcove?

''I checked the closet,'' Antonio said softly, reaching past her to open the door himself. ''Where do you keep it?''

''Under those blankets, up there in the far corner.''

Antonio pushed aside the woven fabric, felt his fingers butt up against steel and pulled out a nine-millimeter Beretta. Light, balanced, a sweet piece of weaponry. The clip was loaded but not pushed all the way in. This wasn't some dinky ladies' gun. This little honey meant business.

''Do you know how to use it?''

''Yes. Daddy's a retired police officer. I grew up around guns.''

''Good.'' He put the Beretta back where he'd found it. ''In the meantime, I think you ought to place a call to your detective friend. See if there's any news.''

''You're right.'' She moved to the nightstand beside the bed and removed a business card, then picked up the extension phone. "Though I'm a little surprised he hasn't called me."

Chelsa waited for the connection to go through, then asked for Mitch's extension. Antonio's supportive hand on her shoulder reminded her that she wasn't alone. She relaxed her death grip on the receiver.

"D'Ambra."

"Mitch? It's Chelsa Lawrence." She heard the hinges on his chair squeak and pictured the handsome detective coming to attention.

"You okay, darlin'?"

His smooth Southern drawl could be deceiving, make a person think he was laid-back. He used it to his advantage—to the misfortune of more than one wily perp. The man was smart as a tack. "I'm not sure. Have you heard anything about Rick's release?"

"No. I've got a request for notification, but sometimes these things get overlooked. I can call right now, if you like."

"I think you'd better. I think he's been here, Mitch." She told him about the unlocked door and the quarter, even though, in the retelling, her fears sounded paper-thin and ungrounded.

The detective swore, then apologized, then swore again, making Chelsa smile despite the graveness of the circumstances. He never questioned her suspicions; he automatically believed her. That was something she appreciated about him. He'd never once accused her of being an overwrought ex-wife. From day one, he'd taken her concerns and intuitions seriously.

Just like Antonio did.

"I'll call right now. Hell, I'll go over there myself. Damn it, how could this have happened? San Alegra's so remote, I thought you'd be safe. How the hell could he find you?''

His rambling was more of a one-sided conversation that didn't require answers or explanations. Although the tone of his queries didn't invite participation, Chelsa responded anyway. ''Rick's a con artist, Mitch. If he wants information bad enough, he'll get it.''

''Very few people know where you are, though. And those who do are people I'd trust with my life—and yours. I don't see how your whereabouts could have leaked.''

''I might be making something out of nothing, Mitch.'' The tense silence on the other end of the line told her he didn't believe that any more than she did. ''To be on the safe side, though, would you look in on my parents?''

''I'll do that right after I check with the prison. In the meantime, stick close to the phone. I'll call you back and make arrangements to get you some protection.''

''That's not necessary. I'm…uh, I'm not alone.''

''Who's with you?'' His voice was like a sharp report of a pistol, full of demand and protectiveness.

''Antonio Castillo.''

A beat of silence. ''*The* Antonio Castillo? The Casanova prince?''

She grinned and cut her gaze to Antonio, who appeared ready to chew nails because he was only hearing one side of the conversation. ''One and the same.''

''I'll be a son of a gun. Are you comfortable with him there?''

Comfortable wasn't exactly the word she'd use, especially with the giddy way her stomach flipped every time she looked at him. Like now. His shirt was hanging open—thanks to her grip that had sent another button scattering—and the sight of that masculine chest covered with dark, enticing hair, gave her hormones a healthy surge that pulsed straight to her feminine core. "Yes, I feel…safe."

"Put him on the phone."

"Really, Mitch—"

"Humor me, darlin'."

She hesitated, nearly hissed, then turned and held the receiver out to Antonio. "He wants to talk to you."

"Good." He took the phone from her. "Antonio Castillo, here."

"Mitch D'Ambra, Vicksburg P.D. I assume you're up to speed on Ms. Lawrence's history?"

"I am."

"What's your take on the situation?"

"Hard to say. I know the people here on the island, and I haven't seen any strangers. We've had a storm and the ferry hasn't made a run, but that's not to say a private boat hasn't pulled up on the beach somewhere."

"I've got people stationed in Barcelona and Cole Martinez is covering the Valldorian port. But you're right—slipups occur. Are you armed?"

"Yes." At least he was now. With Chelsa's Beretta.

"Do you have a problem with staying until I run down a few leads and get a handle on the whereabouts of Rick Lawrence?"

"No problem. Right now, you would not budge me with dynamite."

Mitch D'Ambra gave a sigh that had Antonio frowning. "Yeah, she's that kind of lady. Makes a man want to just wrap her up and take off running. Rick Lawrence is a first-class fool."

"On that we are in agreement."

"Okay. I appreciate your help. I'll call as soon as I have news."

"Call before that. News or not, I insist on being informed."

"You got it."

Antonio replaced the receiver and turned to Chelsa. She had a mutinous expression on her face.

"What?" he asked, bewildered.

"I just want to go on record as having said I don't appreciate that sort of male muscle flexing, or bonding, or whatever that was."

Ah, the lady and he had quite a bit in common. She, too, liked to remain in control. And it set her off that D'Ambra had asked to speak with him...as though she were the weaker sex.

He made an effort to control his grin, and failed. "I don't know D'Ambra well enough to bond, and as for muscle flexing, I assure you, I did no such thing."

She made a sound of disgust deep in her throat. "You know what I meant."

He sobered, stepped up to her and pushed a wayward strand of honey-colored hair behind her ear.

"Yes, *querida,* I know. There was no disrespect intended, nor feelings on either part that you are incapable of conducting your own affairs. However, a good detective can discern a lot from hearing another man speak. He was merely taking my measure, making sure a wily fox was not guarding the hen house."

She gave him a look so astonished, he felt like a

cad. Her disbelief was no less than he deserved. After all, the papers delighted in exploiting his prowess.

"Shame on you, Chelsa. We were speaking about the safety of your person, not your virtue. And on that score, the only promise I will make is that I always wait until I am invited before I pounce."

He knew he got to her by the way her sexy mouth opened and closed, by the way she twisted her hands together. At last, she simply shook her head.

"I'm not even going to touch that statement about my virtue." Her voice trembled, charming him. "I've got to get some work done or the water babies are going to drown under breach of contract."

He watched her leave the room, and although he knew he shouldn't loiter in her bedroom—his imagination was active enough as it was—he also knew he needed to make another call. And it would best be done privately so as not to alarm the children.

This latest turn of events told him the heat was turning up. He hated to see her jump every time the phone rang or look for danger around every corner. And he believed her when she said someone had been in the house. The fact that it had happened right under their noses made his gut twist in anger and frustration.

He disliked sitting on the sidelines, waiting for something to happen, at the mercy of others for action or information. It made him feel impotent that he was forced to do so now—and that particular description, even metaphorically, was horrifying in the extreme for a Latin lover!

The line connected and a woman answered, her voice sultry with an underlying hint of sass. Raquel Santiago Martinez. He grinned.

"Rocky? What are you doing answering the main line of the Royal Guard?"

"Tony! It is so good to hear your voice. News has traveled of your shipwreck. And you must tell me *all* about the woman who has rescued you."

His stomach churned as Raquel's words planted an inkling of suspicion in his mind. He'd called the palace when the phone lines had been restored, forgetting how fast any news involving him would travel. No telling how the story had been embellished, and by whom.

The staff was normally discreet, but that wasn't to say they didn't converse among themselves, or with family members outside the palace, who in turn might tell other friends.

And though Cole Martinez did background checks on everyone they employed, it was impossible to know every detail or connection of every single citizen in Valldoria.

¡Dios! Had he inadvertently been the one to leak Chelsa's whereabouts? Now, more than ever, he wanted answers and action.

Although Raquel's questions were good-natured—and the norm between the two of them—he didn't want to get into the subject of Chelsa right now. At least not with the slant of a playboy wooing the latest woman.

"You did not answer my original question, *mi bella.*"

"Oh, my receptionist duties." She didn't press him on the issue of Chelsa. Raquel was like a sister to him and respected his privacy. "Much has changed, my friend. I am convincing my husband that I can be quite an asset to him."

Antonio heard a masculine grumble in the background. Cole Martinez, head of the Royal Guard, was a stickler for rules and regulations. A quiet, intense man, he'd been a friend of Antonio's since boyhood and secretly in love with Raquel Santiago for almost that long. Now they were happily married, and Antonio suspected Raquel was having the time of her life keeping him off balance—and Cole was having the time of his life keeping up an appearance of bluster, when anyone with a set of eyes knew he would indulge his wife in anything.

"I have no doubt you are an asset to him, Rocky. And a very sexy one I might add."

"I'm not talking about sex! Oh!" She giggled, and there was static on the line as though a friendly scuffle were taking place. "My big strong husband is turning a little green. Did you know he thought you and I had a thing going, Antonio? Oops, I must run. The brute is horribly territorial over the royal phone...."

"Flirting with my wife, again, Tony?" Cole asked.

"Ah, no, *amigo*. I would not dream of such a thing. I make it a point to steer clear of ladies whose husbands wear terrifying guns."

"Still full of it, I see. Is there a reason for the call, buddy?"

Antonio sobered, all kidding aside. Cole Martinez was the best in the business when it came to protection and law enforcement. And he had access to information even agents with top-secret security clearance couldn't get their hands on.

"Yes. I need a favor. I need information and manpower. There is a woman at risk and I will not allow the danger to touch her." He told his friend the whole story, and relayed the conversation he'd had with the detective.

He could hear computer keys already tapping. "D'Ambra's a good man," Cole said. "We trained together in the military and I'd trust him at my back without question. But you're right, he's too far away to ensure the kind of protection you need."

"You are well aware of the case involving Rick Lawrence?"

"Intimately aware. Several of the ship workers here got caught up in the scam, and I took a personal interest in the case because *Don* Carlos asked me to intervene on behalf of his employees." Not to mention that the powerful Carlos Santiago was his father-in-law.

Martinez swore. "There's a glitch in the computer somewhere. It's not letting me access the Mississippi penitentiary. I'll try another avenue." The beep of high-tech machinery sounded like alarms going off. "Come on, baby, put out for me."

Antonio couldn't pass up the opportunity to tease. "Really, my friend, I am terribly fond of you, but I'm not at all sure that is appropriate. Especially since your wife is no doubt listening. And if you but ask her, she will vouch for my gender preferences."

"You're a barrel of laughs, Prince." His mind obviously on seducing his computer to do his bidding, Cole said, "If Lawrence is in the area, that gives me jurisdiction, and believe me, our justice system is much less tolerant than in the States. That's one of the reasons Mrs. Lawrence was sent here."

Antonio frowned at the satisfaction in Cole's tone. "Are you telling me, you hoped he'd show? That you used Chelsa and her daughters as bait?"

Cole hesitated. "Not bait, exactly. There were no guarantees that he would indeed pursue her. On the off chance, though, it is better for all that it happens here."

"Then why the hell did you send her to San Alegra? I have been here several days and no *policia* have conducted rounds of surveillance. She is isolated in this bungalow, just yards from the water where any private boat can come ashore. *¡Madre de Dios!* What were you thinking?"

"We are monitoring the waters, Tony," Cole said. "The very remoteness of the island is protection in itself."

"Perhaps you have misjudged, my friend. The bungalow has been breached—"

"You can't be sure."

His gut fisted into a knot. He felt as though his *own* word had been challenged. "I trust Chelsa's instincts. That gives me certainty. And that being the case, someone has fallen asleep on watch. I myself sailed these waters and was not stopped or questioned."

"Think, Tony. No one would stop the *Diablo Plata.*"

"Which is foolish. Who's to say I was not knocked over the head by pirates and my yacht stolen?" He was merely making a point. His pride wouldn't let him truly entertain such an occurrence.

"I'm as dedicated to this case as you are," Cole said quietly. "I'll have both answers and action for you by morning."

Antonio felt a punch of guilt for taking his frustrations out on a friend. "I appreciate it. And I apologize 'or coming on so strong."

"No problem. I know what it's like to lose objectivity when it's someone you care about. I went through the same thing when Raquel was in trouble. I'll get back to you.''

Antonio replaced the phone, frowning. Yes, he might have lost objectivity because Chelsa was involved, and because he cared what happened to her. But that was it.

Cole, however, had inferred deeper emotions, likening them to those he'd had with Raquel. But Cole had been in love with the heiress.

This wasn't the same situation at all.

Dios. Had he given the impression that it was?

Chapter Eight

Chelsa was having trouble with her latest story. It was difficult to concentrate on sweet emotions and upstanding morals when her mind was constantly in a state of anticipation, waiting for the evil shoe to drop, wondering if she could keep her daughters safe.

Giving up for the time being, she walked into the living room. After Antonio had called his friend in Valldoria, he'd offered to keep the girls occupied so Chelsa could get some work done.

It appeared that Emily and Sophie were the ones doing the occupying. She paused just inside the doorway, watching, her heart going soft at the sight of the three of them on the sofa. The girls looked so small snuggled next to him. It was a perfect family picture, but Prince Antonio Castillo didn't mesh with her everyday images of a father. He was too...well, she couldn't actually come up with the proper word. He was beyond handsome, and had such a presence.

Both Emily and Sophie were vying for his attention, interrupting one another in the telling of a story. It was impossible to wallow in the dumps around Antonio and her children. Just when she was about to succumb to a pity party, one of them would surprise her into laughter…or in Antonio's case, giddy thrills.

Like now, when he looked up and saw her standing in the doorway. His gaze caressed her, held her, made her feel feminine and pretty and desirable. Her stomach tingled and fluttered when he flashed his deep, sexy-as-sin dimples, stealing her breath.

"And the granddaddy said, 'Well, Toots…'"

Antonio was aware of Sophie's little voice, but his concentration had turned to mush. Seeing Chelsa in the doorway, backlit with soft light glancing off her wheat-colored hair, blanked his mind of everything but her. The utter distraction surprised him. He'd never met a woman who could hold him spellbound by just walking into a room, steal his every thought. The fact that she could scared him.

"Toots?" he asked, trying to bring his attention back to the kids' storytelling.

"Yep." Sophie smacked her lips together and nodded, sending her riot of curls bobbing.

But like a magnet, his eyes were drawn once more to Chelsa. Her simple summer dress skimmed her body and fell to her ankles. There was very little shape to the garment, yet on Chelsa it looked sexy and tempting.

Much too tempting for his peace of mind. He swore softly.

The sound of a soft indrawn breath had him looking back down at his storytellers. Sophie's eyes were solemn and round, Emily's were impish and flirty.

"You said a bad word," Sophie whispered, scandalized.

Chelsa's fault, he decided, determined not to get

sidetracked again. "Yes, I did," he said to Sophie. "What is the penalty for such a crime?"

"Well, da water babies hafta eat soap, then da water gets 'taminated.''

"Contaminated?"

"Yep. S'what I said. The water gets 'taminated wif the bubbles cuz the soap washes the bad words all out."

"Nasty. I suppose the baby has to get out of the water?"

"Nope. She has to sit on the lily pad and think about it. And when she learns the lesson and won't say bad stuff no more, the 'taminated bubbles dis go 'way.''

"Just like that?"

"Yep."

Wouldn't life be easy if bad things could be washed away so easily? He suspected there were bad things in Chelsa's life that would take more than a bar of soap to cleanse away, hurts that made her wary to trust.

To trust a man.

It said something about her as a mother that her little girls didn't share her fears and distrust. Obviously she'd done a good job shielding them.

He looked back at Chelsa as she came all the way into the room. The kids followed his gaze.

"Aw," Emily complained. "Is it bedtime already? Can't we stay up longer?"

Her smile was gentle as she eased down on the couch and nodded.

The kids scrambled over the top of Antonio, pouncing on Chelsa, snuggling into her arms, and for some reason, Antonio envied that profound love and closeness.

¡Dios! Had the knock on his head altered his personality? The very thought shook him up.

"Did you do a new story?" Emily asked.

"Yeah, you could read it and we could 'teak it.'"

"Teak?" Antonio interrupted. He'd gotten pretty adept at translating Sophie's words, but this one stumped him.

"Critique," Chelsa clarified. "I usually read my work in progress and use the girls as sounding boards. If the story won't hold their interest, it'll bomb with other children, too. Emily and Sophie are my staunchest critiquers." She looked back at the girls. "And no, I didn't get very far on my story today. I'm having some trouble concentrating."

"We could help."

"Thanks sweetie, but Momma's brain is mush right now. Maybe tomorrow, we'll start fresh."

Antonio winked. "If we are arranging work schedules, I feel I must ask a question of the goddess and little mermaid." He schooled his features into absolute seriousness. "I am assuming you have negotiated an equitable percentage of royalties?"

They all frowned at him and it took considerable control to keep from blowing the act by laughing.

"Ah, I can see you need an agent to attend to your best interests. Perhaps we can negotiate…say, one piece of candy each before bed?"

"Yeah!" the girls chorused, leaping off the couch and bobbing up and down like a couple of Mexican jumping beans.

"Really, Tony," Chelsa admonished. "Sugar this close to bedtime isn't such a good—"

"Nonsense. Any time is good for candy." He stood. "Do not move an inch," he said to the girls. Chelsa would forgive this one indulgence. If he gave away the hiding place they'd found for the bakery bag, it would be another matter.

FORTIFIED with a small piece of chocolate, the girls went to bed with little fuss. It worried Chelsa that they'd insisted on Antonio coming along to tuck them in. Was she setting them up for hurt once it came time for her to go home and Antonio to go on with his life? That was a very real possibility, but for the time being, she selfishly hoarded his attention. Emily and Sophie were starved for male companionship and Antonio was more than willing to hand it out.

Now, without the buffer of the children, Chelsa grew nervous. Obviously, *she* was just as starved for male attention.

She felt Antonio's gaze on her as she picked up scattered toys and straightened the clutter in the front room.

He surprised her by pitching in to help. This unorthodox prince definitely kept her off balance.

"Sit with me," he invited once there wasn't so much as a piece of lint out of place.

Oh, she wanted to do more than sit. The scene was set with soft lighting and the romantic sound of surf rolling against the shore. She reined in her runaway hormones, and complied, picking up her sketch book as a means of distraction, a means of occupying her mind so it didn't wander to the fact that they were basically alone.

"So, you are having trouble with your stories?"

Evidently he wasn't appreciating the intimacy of

the setting as she was. Feeling foolish, she firmly squashed her thoughts.

"A little. Probably just the stress of the day."

"Understandable." He touched her hair, then drew his hand back as though the action hadn't been intended. "Perhaps I can be of service?"

Absolutely, she thought. *Oh, Chelsa, get your mind off the man's zipper!* "And will you demand royalties also?"

"I am as easily satisfied as Emily and Sophie. Something sweet, perhaps." His gaze focused on her lips, his dark eyes so hot, she nearly melted.

"Tony..." she warned.

"Just a thought. Okay. Story ideas. How about a battalion of doodlebugs arriving in marching formation to save the water babies from being blown up by the evil octopus?"

"I don't write about violence."

"Ah, no violence. The doodlebugs will prevent the disaster and shame the giant squid in the process."

Her mind working, she pictured the scene, automatically drawing a quick sketch of tiny bugs sporting antenna and armed with water cannons. "It could work," she mused, feeling her creativity begin to flow. "It would show that the little guy can win over the big ones."

"Yes." His enthusiasm told her he was really getting into the spirit of things. "In the absence of ammo, you're using water. The bad octopus won't blow up the babies' habitat because this particular species of octopi are disintegrated by water. The doodlebugs have the advantage because their squirt guns are scary and can reduce the tentacled creatures to inky puddles."

She slanted him an arched look. "You're sneaking up on the side of violence again."

He grinned. "Can't help it. As a kid, I was fixated on blowing stuff up."

"Your poor mother."

"Actually, she preferred my chemistry experiments to purloining a greenhouse full of her prized orchids."

"A whole greenhouse full?"

His grin was sheepish. "Now that I think of it, that might have been a bit excessive."

"A bit. What did you do with them?"

"Decorated my yacht. I was wooing a budding actress."

She smiled and shook her head, sketching the evil octopi with artillery strapped to their stringy arms and masks over their dome-shaped heads.

"Now, that's my kind of firepower," he said, his shoulder brushing hers as he leaned closer to have a look.

"They're duds," she defended, her mind conjuring an entirely different kind of firepower. His breath was warm against her neck, and he smelled so masculine. The lines on the paper squiggled as her hand trembled and her heart pounded. He was so close. All it would take was a mere shift of her body and she'd be in his arms.

And she wanted that in the worst way.

To distract herself, she said, "You're blowing my image of what royal families are supposed to act like. Was your brother as incorrigible as you?"

"Ah, no. Joseph had his moments, but duty was always uppermost in his mind. Until he met Briana."

"He started blowing things up then?"

"No. But he outdid me in wooing techniques. Although he left mother's gardens alone, he bought out nearly every flower shop from France to America.''

''That's romantic.''

''Yes. I did not think he had it in him. But he fell in love and there was no stopping him. It has pleased me to see the change in him. They have just had a baby—Joseph Lorenzo II. And since it is a boy, he will be next in line for the throne.''

''Somehow that doesn't seem right. Does it bother you?''

''Not at all. I do not want any part of what Joseph has—at least in the respect of duty. Joseph is the ambassador of goodwill. I am content to be the ambassador of fun.'' He scooted closer, his hand covering hers against the sketchpad, turning the tablet so he could get a better look at the armed octopi.

Chelsa had thought conversation would ease the sensual turmoil inside her. She'd been wrong.

With the slight touch of his hand, he set off tremors inside of her, ignited her fantasies.

She stood abruptly. ''I think I'll go to bed.''

He looked confused by her abrupt announcement, and she didn't give him the opportunity to talk her out of it. That would be all too easy and entirely too dangerous.

''Night, Tony. Thanks for the inspiration.''

''My pleasure.''

And hers. Before her mind could stray even further, she fled.

Once in her bedroom, though, she was at loose ends. She wasn't sleepy; her nerves were too tense. Anticipation shimmered in the balmy air of the room like the hum of a taut violin string. She longed to open the window and let the soft ocean breeze cool her overheated skin, but she didn't dare.

Lord, she was lonely. And although Antonio was the wrong man for her, she could feel her resistance weakening, feel the ache rising like high tide, washing over her, making her yearn to throw caution to the wind, to go back in the front room and beg for what his hot eyes said he'd be more than willing to give.

Feeling as though she were a giant mass of ultra-sensitive emotions, she switched on the portable disc player and adjusted the volume. Country-and-western music whispered softly from the speakers. Dear heaven, the chemistry between her and Antonio was unmistakable. And so electric, it sparked like sulfurous lightning whenever they got within two feet of one another. It had been so long since she'd let herself feel. For so long she'd had to be both mother and father to her girls; she'd had to be strong, to set aside her own needs.

Now she'd met a man who made her laugh, who kept her on her toes and ignited her deepest fantasies. Since the day Antonio Castillo had literally crashed into her life, she'd found herself thinking about sex at inappropriate moments and longing for steamier ways to work her major muscle groups other than pushing a shopping cart or chasing after her kids.

Restless, unsure what to do with the longing that nearly overpowered her, she picked up Sophie's teddy bear from the window seat. Button eyes stared back at her from the soft furry face.

Suddenly she longed to be young and carefree again, to dance and laugh and love. To not worry about dangers or deranged ex-husbands, or where the money for groceries was going to come from, or whether or not her creativity would dry up and send her career plummeting.

The soft strains of Wynonna Judd drifted out of the stereo speakers. Holding the teddy bear in a semblance of a correct waltz position, she began to move her feet to the sultry beat.

Antonio heard the music and paused outside Chelsa's bedroom door. It wasn't closed all the way, and after a brief tussle with his conscience, he pushed the door open. He was drawn to this woman in a way he couldn't explain.

She moved across the hardwood floor, keeping a slow, three-step time, like a laid-back waltz. In her arms was a teddy bear.

His blood heated.

She should have looked silly. Instead, she looked incredibly erotic, her eyes closed, her hand holding the furry paw of the stuffed toy, her hips swaying, her bare feet caressing the floor. He could stand there all night and just watch.

No, he couldn't. He wanted to participate. He wanted to hold her in his arms, to feel the press of her soft curves against his body, to have that dreamy look on her face be because of *him.*

Chelsa wasn't sure what broke into her subconscious. But suddenly she knew she wasn't alone. The feeling wasn't one of fear or danger. At least not the danger she'd been living with for the past months.

She stopped abruptly and opened her eyes.

And couldn't move a muscle.

Antonio stepped into the room, his stride purposeful, intent etched in his handsome features. She felt silly for being caught dancing with a stuffed teddy bear, but the fervid pounding of her heart washed away the embarrassment.

His gaze held her, softly, intensely, as he tapped the stuffed toy on its furry shoulder.

"Pardon me, sir, may I cut in?"

His Latin accent was even more pronounced with the very softness of his voice. His eyes never wavered from hers.

Barely aware of the movement, she nodded her head. Dear Lord, it was what she wanted, and at the moment, she was blinded to any valid reason why she shouldn't simply indulge herself, to lose herself in his eyes and his touch and his easygoing, exquisitely thrilling essence, to let him breathe life back into her own battered spirit. Was that so wrong?

His arms slid around her, firmly, holding her against the heat of his body. There was no hesitation, only a male sureness that mesmerized, left little room for second thoughts. Their bodies touched from her breasts to her knees, sending desire on a raging course through her veins.

A perfect fit, she thought dimly, even though he was a good head taller.

Her feet moved in time with his as Wynonna sang of hopeless love and reckless passion.

And oh, she was feeling that passion. In the deepest part of her mind—the rational part—she knew she should question it, but she didn't.

"You are so lovely," he whispered. *"Magnifico."*

"So are you."

His brow arched. She might have laughed at the gaucheness of her statement if she weren't so breathless. His palm seared her back, low on her waist, his fingers resting just above the swell of her buttocks.

Her breasts pressed against his chest, her nipples aching with the need to be caressed.

Only with Antonio had she ever responded so wantonly.

"We shouldn't be doing this." Her voice was a mere breath of sound, yet her feet never paused in the beat of the music, nor did she draw away from his arms.

"We should be doing exactly this...and more."

His lips pressed tenderly against her forehead, her nose, over her cheek.

Frustration built. Her own lips felt swollen from wanting. And he was moving entirely too slow, taking his time, savoring. An ideal man by most women's standards, but she wasn't feeling like most women right now. And a slow touch wasn't what she wanted.

Taking matters into her own hands, she lifted her face, burying her fingers in his silky hair, urging him to taste, to take, to give and to receive.

The touch of his lips against hers was like fire and ice, shocking her to her core. Oh, how she wanted, and the wanting was a fierceness that knew no conscience.

The tip of his tongue caressed the seam of her lips, asking for—and receiving—entrance.

And again she understood the draw of this Latin lover. Expertise was an understatement. He kissed her like she'd never been kissed before, tapping into emotions she'd never felt before. He wasn't a man to stay, had indeed warned her to guard her heart, but right now she didn't care. All she cared about was this— this feeling. This thrilling, exquisite feeling.

Her feet no longer moved to the plaintive rhythm

of the country music. Instead, she moved to a beat of her own—the pulse of her femininity.

The yearning grew, gaining momentum, spiraling out of control. She wanted to climb right up his body. Her need to be one with him drove her. She couldn't get close enough, and the frustration was almost pain.

"Easy, *querida*."

She moaned, maybe even begged. At this point, she couldn't be sure.

"Are you sure?"

His question seemed echoed her thoughts. Then she realized it was born of her actions. She'd already given him the go-ahead with her body. Now he wanted the words.

"Yes."

Even as she gave the permission, he was backing her slowly toward the bed, lowering her to the mattress, following her down. The press of his weight made her ache all the more. The cotton of her dress was so thin, it might as well have been nonexistent.

Her legs parted, making room for him, cradling him in the juncture of her thighs. Through his jeans she felt his arousal pressing against the part of her that ached for fulfillment.

Antonio slipped the spaghetti strap from her shoulder, eager to taste her, raining kisses over each smooth inch of skin he uncovered. She smelled of citrus and tasted like a dream. Her breath was coming hard and fast, driving him on. He'd always prided himself on his control, but with Chelsa, he was fast learning that he'd given himself entirely too much credit.

Because she was shattering his control as easily as the rocky shoreline had shattered his boat.

Astonished, he noticed that his hands shook as he lowered the top of her dress, exposed her breasts.

"It drives me crazy when you wear these T-shirt dresses with no bra."

"Don't talk," she said, breathless.

"Why?"

"Because I can't concentrate."

"Ah, *bella,* I will teach you."

"I'm going to teach you in a minute if you don't hurry up." She fumbled with his shirt, popping another button.

He chuckled, surprised he had breath to do so. This woman astonished him with her avidness. "Good thing I have purchased additional shirts."

"In that case…" She gave a tug and ripped the rest of the buttons, sending them scattering across the mattress.

For a moment he went utterly still, stunned. He could not recall a woman ever stunning him before…or charming him so.

"I've called Sophie the mermaid. I think I have it wrong. You are the siren."

She placed her fingers over his lips, sending a wash of heat through his veins. And he knew it was no longer time for words.

So he spoke with his touch, and with his lips. Slowly. Though it was killing him to exercise the restraint. He wanted nothing more than to plunder, to test her inhibitions, then banish them. He wanted to find out how far and how fast he could take her—or she could take him.

With the bodice of her dress around her waist, bare skin teasing bare skin, he ran his hand along her thigh, inching her hemline upward, intensely concentrated on her pleasure, on their shared goal.

He felt her stiffen and his hand stilled.

"What is it, *querida?*" He'd lost her attention.

She squirmed from beneath him. "Emily."

"What?" Confusion colored the single word, yet he automatically moved off her, gave her room.

"Emily's crying." She snatched the straps of her dress back up to her shoulders. "I have to go to her. She has nightmares."

Desire barely ebbing, he followed her out of the room.

Emily was crying and thrashing, yet her eyes were closed.

Chelsa eased onto the bed beside her daughter and gathered her in her arms. "It's okay, sweetheart. Momma's here. Momma's here."

Antonio hovered by the door, unsure what to do. He watched Emily's skinny arms wrap around her mother's neck. Her eyes were open now, wild and unfocused. Then clarity flickered like the click of a camera. "Don't let him find us, Momma."

"Oh, honey. You mustn't worry. It was only a dream."

"But you were scared, and I was scared, and so was Sophie."

"It was only a dream," she repeated, stroking Emily's mussed hair. Dear Lord, these children were too young to know about fear. "No one is going to hurt us."

"Promise?"

"I promise." *Please, God, don't let me break that promise.* Her throat ached with unshed tears, tears she couldn't allow to fall. She had to be strong, had to be *stronger*.

Obviously she'd failed miserably in shielding her daughter. Sophie was young and in her own world, and appeared not to understand most of what was going on. Even now, she slept like an angel, blissfully unaware of her sister's torment. But Emily had picked up on the unease, had overheard conversations no six-year-old should hear.

And for that, Chelsa had huge regrets.

She also had regrets for the way she'd behaved tonight with Antonio. Selfishly she'd thought to take something for herself, to appease a physical ache, to give in to passion and feel like a woman—not as a mother, or a career woman, or a fearful ex-wife on the run, but a woman. Feminine. Desirable. Carefree enough to seize the moment.

But at what expense? In retrospect—and with a room's length between them—she realized that the expense was way beyond her modest reach. She couldn't allow herself to get in deeper with Antonio Castillo.

She glanced over the top of her daughter's head, her eyes meeting his.

This man could break her heart.

She had enough to deal with, her children had enough to deal with. She needed to remember that.

Yet the sight of him hesitating in the doorway made it difficult.

And even more so when Emily noticed him there, too.

"Momma, can you and Antonio come and sleep with me so I won't be scared?"

Oh, dear. This was going to get sticky.

Antonio came all the way into the room and sat on the edge of the mattress. When Emily unwound her arms from Chelsa's neck and scooted next to him, Chelsa felt bereft, and a little jealous. At least she told herself that's what she was feeling. She wouldn't admit that the sight of her daughter now clinging to Antonio gave her hope wings.

Wings of wanting and "what ifs" and wishes.

Wings she'd better make a stronger effort to clip.

"I do not believe the three of us will fit in this small twin bed, *diosa*. How about if I promise to sit right here until you fall asleep?"

"But what if the bad dream comes back?"

"It would not dare. There is a rule about bad dreams. Only one allowed a night. And I think we must make an addition to that rule and insist they will not be tolerated at all, on any night."

Emily giggled. "You can't make rules about dreams, silly. They don't have ears."

"They most certainly do. Cute little dainty ears. And they will listen if we speak to them just right." He bent close, whispering in Emily's ear.

Chelsa felt as though a thousand tiny butterflies had taken flight in her stomach. Here was this reputed Latin lover—a playboy prince—soothing a little girl's fears...banishing monsters like any loving father would do.

She closed her eyes against both the sight and the thought.

He wasn't father material. He was a rolling stone. Carefree and out for fun.

And she was terribly overwrought to be reading more into his actions than was actually there.

Chapter Nine

The conversation at the breakfast table was lively, and Emily didn't seem to be suffering any ill effects from her nightmare.

Chelsa couldn't say she'd fared as well.

She'd slept poorly, felt hot and sticky and, damn it, still humming with desire. If Emily hadn't interrupted them last night, would she be dealing with the dreaded morning-after nerves?

Good night, her mind was stuck in a groove. All she could think about was that she needed to shave her legs, cream her skin…take a *cold* shower!

And therein lay her dilemma. Normally she didn't lock the bathroom door and the kids came in and out at will. With a man in the house though—a man she was seriously attracted to—it wouldn't do to have the door swinging open at inopportune moments.

Still, she couldn't leave the girls unattended.

Wanting to reach out and touch that silky lock of dark hair that flopped sexily over Antonio's brow, she linked her fingers together instead.

"Uh…Antonio?"

His gaze honed in on her, making her heart pound. "Yes?"

"Could you, um…watch the girls for me while I shower?" Honestly, engaging a prince as a baby-sitter!

He grinned. "Need help washing your back?"

The girls thought that was hysterically funny. Thank goodness they were too young to realize the very real adult challenge in his tone.

"I think I can handle it," she said primly and fled. He hadn't actually agreed, but she trusted him.

When had that happened?

Locking the bathroom door, she whipped her sleep shirt over her head. Running her palm over her legs, she nearly screamed in mortification. She'd been half-naked with a man last night and the hair on her legs resembled an overgrown forest. Well, a patchy meadow, maybe, but still.

Armed with scented soap and a new razor blade, she stepped into the shower, telling herself she was exercising good hygiene for her own benefit—*not* out of anticipation of Antonio Castillo getting close enough again to feel the stubble on her legs!

ANTONIO POURED a cup of coffee from the carafe. The kids were chasing Señor Gatito, giggling as the cat batted at the spongy ball they tossed back and forth for the feline's entertainment.

He paused in midsip as Chelsa came into the kitchen, her enticing citrus scent filling the room, wrapping around him, making him ache to touch and taste her.

Nothing smelled better, or was more alluring, than a woman right after a bath.

He stepped closer, to enjoy, to appreciate, but the

shrill of the phone thwarted his intentions—and sent his gut twisting into knots.

¡Dios! He wanted to jerk the instrument out of the wall, hated the way terror washed over Chelsa, the way her peaches-and-cream cheeks lost their color.

"Let me," he said quietly as the telephone gave another peal.

She shook her head and reached for the receiver. She might have been caught off guard, but he could see the core of steel raising its shield, squaring her shoulders.

He didn't bother to hide the fact that he was eavesdropping, or that he was ready to take the phone from her if the call upset her. But by the tone of the conversation, he could tell it was a business call. He frowned. How many people had this number?

Her parents, perhaps? The detective, certainly, as well as Cole. And his own family more than likely.

In his opinion, that was too many and not at all safe.

When she hung up, he waited patiently for her to share the caller's identity. His curiosity surprised him. For a man who lived by the motto Live And Let Live, he'd become awfully embroiled in Chelsa Lawrence's life.

"That was my agent," she said. A sort of ethereal excitement emanated from her, yet he could tell she was suppressing it.

"I am wondering if it is wise to give out this number."

She shrugged. "I'm under contract, so it's necessary. Besides, Rick doesn't know about my publisher, or Melody, my agent."

They hoped. "There is good news for you?"

She licked her lips, causing his heart to slam against his ribs. Then she picked up a sponge and wiped at nonexistent streaks on the counter.

"A tentative offer. A children's TV network wants me to do a treatment for a new series they have in the works. An ongoing cartoon."

"This is a good thing, is it not?" Why wasn't she leaping about the room? Why did he detect hesitation?

"It could be. They're offering big money, and *that* I can certainly use."

"But?" he asked, prodding her to voice her reserve.

"But it's not a good time for me. My life's topsy-turvy at the moment. I have to think about the girls, about anonymity. I told Melody that I couldn't commit right now, to stall them."

"This sounds like a wonderful opportunity for you. You have a gift, Chelsa. Think of all the children you could reach with your message of morals and honesty through the medium of television."

"It's too risky." She squeezed the sponge, then abandoned it altogether.

"Are you certain it would draw undue attention to you?"

"Any new venture that involves this kids' network has the potential to wind up in the business section of the newspaper. Besides, I have to wonder if I could do a script justice with the turmoil my mind is in lately." Her lips turned up in what should have resembled a smile. "Look at the trouble I've had with this latest book. I'll have to add your name to the contract as collaborator if my ideas don't start flowing soon."

"You are selling yourself short."

Her smile vanished. "No. What I am is scared."

He reached for her without thought, brought her to his chest and just held her. *Madre de Dios,* he wanted to shelter this woman, protect her, ease her burdens and pave her world with rose petals. Make it right. Fix it.

That notion was so far removed from the person he'd known himself to be for the last twenty-nine— almost thirty—years, that it made him uneasy.

"You cannot hide forever. Precautions are necessary, certainly, but you must live your life."

"That's easy for you to say." Chelsa stepped back from his hold. She'd wanted to jump on the offer; even now her stomach quivered with giddy excitement. But the timing couldn't have been worse. "You're not in my shoes. I'm not a wimp or a scaredy-cat. I'm responsible for my children. And if there's any question over their safety, I won't chance it. Not at any cost. And especially not to further my career."

He looked like he wanted to say more, but the loud whoop of a helicopter intruded. Adrenaline shot through Chelsa, making her dizzy. She snatched aside the kitchen curtains, her lungs feeling as though they were about to burst.

Breathe, she ordered herself. *Out, then in.*

Emily and Sophie abandoned their game of tag with Señor Gatito and charged into the kitchen, each grabbing a handful of Chelsa's dress.

"What is it, Momma?" Emily asked.

Sophie simply held on, silent, her wide round eyes searching out Antonio.

Although her hands trembled, she rested them on

her daughter's shoulders in reassurance. She hated the way the fear winged out of nowhere, paralyzing her, telegraphing itself to her children. Her job was to protect, to soothe, to remain calm, to shield these young innocents from unnecessary upset. Yet, at the same time, she needed to be smart, to be on guard.

Dear God, how was a mother supposed to balance all those emotions? To hide her own human failings?

Antonio was beside them in an instant, lifting Sophie into his arms and passing his palm gently over Emily's soft cheek, tipping up the little girl's chin. The warmth of his body pressed against Chelsa's side. In one single move he had included the three of them in his protective circle, in the strength of his steadiness.

"The helicopter bears the Valldorian crest," he said softly. "They are my friends. Cole Martinez and his wife, Raquel."

"The one who made the water baby picture?" Sophie asked.

"That is the one."

Chelsa watched as the rotors whipped up a cloud of sand that rained gritty little pings against the window.

When the whine of the motor died and the blades twirled to a stop, a man and woman alighted. Tall and striking, with the dark good looks Chelsa decided every man in Valldoria must possess, Cole Martinez carefully lifted his wife out of the sleek chopper and kept her hand in his as they approached the bungalow.

"Come," Antonio said. "You will like my friends."

Chelsa followed him to the front door. He still held Sophie in one strong arm, and tenderly cupped Emily's hand with his free one. The sight of the three of them made her eyes sting, made her long for a true family unit, something she'd desperately yearned for with Rick, yet had never had.

The loving bickering and whirlwind of activity taking place between Cole and Raquel Martinez, though, captured Chelsa's attention.

"Slow down, spitfire," Cole said to his wife as they mounted the porch steps. "You need to take it easy."

"I am merely pregnant, Cole. Not incapacitated."

Antonio grinned and accepted a warm embrace from Rocky that enveloped the children, as well. Since his hands were occupied with Emily and Sophie, he didn't offer the traditional masculine greeting to Cole, but nodded instead.

"Congratulations, *amigo*. I did not know you were to be a father."

"Neither did I until this morning." He kept a cautious eye on his wife. "Help me out, Tony. Tell her she should be resting."

"Ah, no, my friend. Do not put me in the middle of this. I will, however, ask your permission to kiss the expectant mother."

Cole shot him a dark look. "I suppose you're safe enough, since your hands are occupied. But only on the cheek."

"Oh, he is so stuffy," Raquel said, giggling, pressing her lips in a sisterly fashion square on Antonio's lips.

Cole gave a long-suffering sigh.

Antonio grinned.

"And who are these lovely cherubs?" Raquel asked, touching each little girl's cheek.

"Sophie and Emily Lawrence." Antonio set Sophie on her feet and stepped back, holding out his hand for Chelsa. "And this is their mother, Chelsa Lawrence."

Before Chelsa could even think about accepting Antonio's outstretched hand, Raquel stepped between them, gathering Chelsa into an embrace that might have suggested they'd been longtime friends.

"I am so happy to meet you. You must accept my personal gratitude for saving our wayward prince from a watery grave."

"Ah now, Rapunzel, you *do* exaggerate," Antonio objected. "I am much too accomplished to end up at the bottom of the sea."

Raquel ignored him. To Chelsa, she said, "It is a wonder he can fit his ego within the walls of the bungalow."

Chelsa laughed, deciding right away that she liked this energetic woman. Raquel's stunning beauty alone might have made Chelsa feel inferior, but the heiress's verve and sweetness invited friendship and girl talk and an easiness not many could pull off.

And what a contradiction she was. Her shoulder-length auburn hair was sleek and styled, with chunks of red highlights that caught the sun and turned it to fire. Spitfire, she'd heard Cole call his wife. The nickname fit. She wore skintight, pencil-slim capris that rode low on her hips and a halter top that hugged her breasts and exposed a flat stomach that hadn't yet swollen with the signs of pregnancy.

She was like an exotic, colorful bird, with plenty of sass that was tempered by unmistakable sweetness.

"I'm happy to meet you, too," Chelsa said. "I've wanted to compliment you in person on your work."

Raquel lit up. "You have seen it?"

"I own a piece. Compliments of Antonio, that is. It's the print entitled *Hope.*"

"Ah, yes. That one is special to me."

"You have a good eye for babies."

"Yes I do," she said without an ounce of modesty. "And your little ones are perfect subjects. It is a curse, I think, but I cannot look upon a child and resist the opportunity to photograph them. My mind simply takes off at will. And it is doing so now. May I have your permission to take Sophie and Emily outdoors?"

Chelsa opened her mouth to object, an automatic instinct, but Raquel, impassioned and animated over her subject, barely paused for breath.

"My cameras are in the helicopter and your children would be so perfect captured in print. Oh, those sweet, round cheeks. Please do not say no. I can already picture the shot of them building a sand castle."

Chelsa's nerves screamed a warning. But hadn't she just lectured herself on not transferring her fears to her children? The girls were looking intrigued by the prospect of having their pictures taken.

"I suppose it would be all right. But..."

Raquel laid a hand on Chelsa's arm. "The photographs will be my gift to you alone," she said gently. "Cole has told me of your troubles. I would not compromise your children's safety by allowing their images to become public domain. However, when your bad time is over and forgotten, I might resort to begging for publication rights. I suspect these sweet darlings will be highly photogenic."

"Thank you. Let me just get some shoes."

"No." Again Raquel stopped her with a hand on

her arm. Her voice lowered. "My husband wishes to discuss business. It would be best if the *niñas* are not within earshot."

Chelsa glanced outside, feeling a sense of foreboding that set her on edge. She must have done a good job of hiding it, though, because Emily and Sophie perked right up, tripping over themselves to accompany the beautiful heiress outdoors, each vying for the lion's share of Raquel's attention.

Cole, however, picked up on her unease. "Your children will be safe, Mrs. Lawrence. Johnny Cruz is both my pilot and my second-in-command. He will watch over Raquel and the girls."

"Call me Chelsa," she said absently, still feeling the need to stay within touching distance to her daughters. Just in case...

"Chelsa it is, then. My wife is stubborn about following rules and remaining cooped up inside. And when inspiration strikes to take photographs, there is no stopping her. Johnny will guard them well. I would not take chances with my wife—nor your little girls."

His absolute sincerity and certainty finally broke Chelsa's tension. "Okay." She glanced at Antonio, noticing that he appeared watchful yet easy with the situation. Perhaps she was overreacting.

"Besides," Cole continued, "I truly believe she is dying for special photographs of your children, even if it is killing her soul not to be in here privy to our discussion." He sighed and looked at Antonio. "Raquel has taken it into her head lately that she is part of the Royal Guard."

"Ah, *amigo,*" Antonio said. "You have my sympathies."

"I appreciate at least *somebody* being on my side."

He said it with so much forlorn masculine pride, Chelsa laughed. "It amazes me how quickly she can capture the perfect shot. You wait and see. She will give us only enough time to discuss basics before she returns."

Basics, Chelsa thought. Was there such a thing in connection to her problems? She didn't think so.

Antonio's hand at her back was warm and reassuring as he steered her to the sofa. "Let us sit, *querida*." To Cole he said, "What have you learned?"

Cole chose to remain standing. Although he appeared to give them his sole attention, Chelsa could tell he kept a sharp eye on their surroundings and every movement going on outside.

"You were right. Your ex-husband has been released from jail. And at the moment he is at large. He has failed to check in with his parole officer."

If she'd been standing, she might have fallen. Cole Martinez's words landed like red-hot boulders in her stomach, and it took every ounce of control Chelsa possessed not to charge outside and grab Emily and Sophie, to lock the doors and pull the curtains and simply hide. Her insides quivered so violently, it was a wonder her neck muscles were even capable of holding up her head.

Antonio eased down beside her on the sofa, his arm around her shoulders, lending her much-needed strength.

Cole's gaze sharpened with speculation, but Chelsa didn't bother to worry about how cozy she and Prince Antonio might appear. She had much bigger worries.

"He's here," she said softly, pleased that her voice only shook a little. "Watching." Her stomach twisted. In an act that seemed as natural as breathing, she rested her hand on Antonio's thigh, needing the touch, the reassurance.

"I have men searching the island," Cole said. "So far, they haven't turned up anything. And they're very thorough."

Most likely he'd meant his last statement as reassurance. Chelsa wondered, however, if there wasn't a hint of doubt seeping through. And truthfully she couldn't blame him if maybe a small part of him thought she was overreacting. A 1992 tails-up quarter was flimsy evidence at best. "Rick's sly."

Cole's lips twisted, yet in no way resembled a smile. "I'm slyer. I'll find him."

So he wasn't doubting after all. That much was evident in his tone, and it made her feel better. The last thing she wanted was to appear like an overwrought ninny in front of Antonio's friends.

"What about in the meantime?" Antonio asked.

She felt his warm breath stir the hair at her temple, and knew she shouldn't be snuggled against his side this way, but she stayed where she was.

"In the meantime, I think it's best if Chelsa and her children relocate."

Antonio nodded. "To Valldoria."

"Yes," Cole agreed.

Chelsa looked from one man to the other. Were they out of their minds? She was no one to them. They had no obligation to help her. And she definitely didn't want to be the one to put these royal people in danger.

They'd been lucky so far because San Alegra was fairly remote. Valldoria was another matter entirely. The media would be on Tony the moment he stepped on the soil of his homeland. And anyone who happened to be beside him would be newsworthy, too.

An open invitation for Rick. Like sending a personal invitation via the wire service.

''No.'' She shook her head.

''No?'' Antonio's tone suggested he wasn't used to opposition. ''Think, Chelsa. Anyone can slip by on the ferry, or bring their own boat out to the island. At the palace you would be well guarded.''

As much as she might want to turn her life over to his capable hands, she still shook her head. ''You're too newsworthy, Antonio. The minute you return home, the whole world will know about it—including Rick. And if the kids and I are in tow, that not only puts us in danger, it'll jeopardize you and your family, too.'' The thought of bringing danger to the people of the palace—or to Antonio, was intolerable.

And Chelsa knew exactly where that strong feeling came from. Against her better judgment, she'd fallen in love with Prince Antonio Castillo of Valldoria.

One of the things most important to her was protecting those she loved…even if in this case, the love was hopeless.

He wasn't the staying kind, and she wasn't cut out to be royalty.

Even if fairy tales did come true, even if he *were* the type of man who could fall in love with her, she still couldn't link her life with his. That would be like giving Rick his own personal viewing screen to her life. For as long as she lived, Rick would be able to keep tabs on her and the girls, and Chelsa would never again have a moment's peace. She'd forever be waiting for the other shoe to drop, for the ghosts of her past to spring up around every corner and shout, ''Boo.''

Again she shook her head and whispered, ''No.''

Antonio felt an uncontrollable, uncharacteristic urge to shake this delicate woman. To harness his control, he stood and paced instead, nearly running into Raquel as she came back into the bungalow. For no good reason, that set him off, too. Cole had been right. The heiress did not relish being left out of anything remotely resembling cloak-and-dagger stuff.

¡Dios! For a man who prided himself on knowing women, the ones in his life at the moment were running amok, not adhering to any of the characteristics he figured they should. Stubborn. The both of them. Especially Chelsa.

''I might not recognize my title often, but I do hold a certain amount of power,'' he said, pinning Chelsa with a look that dared her to contradict him. ''I think I've got enough clout to control the local media, and I've sure as hell got enough smarts to get us to the palace unseen. God knows I've slipped in and out often enough without notice.''

The tension in the room became thick enough to cut.

Raquel defused it by sending the girls to search for the cat, then stepped into the middle of the fray.

''I could not help but overhear your objections, Chelsa,'' she said. ''And as much as I wish I could uphold the sisterhood and side with you, I find I must agree with my husband and Tony. The palace is like a fortress. I should know. For too many years I felt stifled by the watchful eyes of security, until one special security guy came along and taught me that love sets you free—but that it's still a good idea to lock the doors.''

Cole glanced at his wife with amused indulgence. ''She's right, Chelsa. The palace is the safest place—even if my own wife was too stubborn to listen to my advice at one time.''

''It was not stubbornness, and you know it,'' Raquel countered, flicking her hair behind her ear and facing her husband as though girded for a battle.

Chelsa might have smiled at the picture they presented, but her own thoughts and emotions were in too much turmoil. It was so difficult to stand firm when everything within her wanted to cave in.

Oh, she should have never let herself fall in love—as if she could have prevented it in the first place, she thought. If she were the cause of harm to Antonio or his family, she could never live with the pain. It was hard enough as it was, knowing the pain she would experience when he left. And she knew he would leave, because Antonio, by his own admission, was a rolling stone with no intention of settling down. The heartache of losing him to wanderlust could be borne, she assured herself.

The pain of losing him to her ex-husband's madness could not.

Startled, she sucked in a breath when Antonio stepped in front of her, gripped her arms and brought her to her feet. The intensity in his brown eyes bored into her like a laser. Determination was tempered by tenderness, though she imagined it cost him some effort.

He held her in front of him for several moments, his eyes never wavering. Their knees bumped, and for a wild moment she though he was going to jerk her the rest of the way to him. Her heart skittered strangely and a throbbing ache pulsed through her. A mere inch and their pelvises would be aligned, pressing...arousing.

She blinked. Good night, what in the world was she thinking?

"Antonio—"

"Hush." His voice was soft and rough edged, and held a command that bespoke his status—even though he denied it half the time. "I am capable of taking care of myself, and my family has an excellent guard to see to their safety. So do not present me with that argument again. If you will not think of yourself, at least think of your children. Can you guarantee their safety?"

She lowered her eyes. Trust him to bring out the big guns. She would do anything, at any cost, to keep her children safe. "No."

"Our Royal Guard can. *I* can." His voice softened, as did his touch. His palms caressed now, rather than held. "Come with me, *querida.*" His fingertips brushed a curl from her cheek. "I owe you for rescuing me from the surf. You must let me return the favor and see you through your crisis."

Oh, there was danger in his touch, in his silky, accented voice, in allowing herself to remain close.

But that danger was only to her heart.

The threat to her life and her children's lives took precedence.

Although there were no guarantees, he *was* offering her a safer haven. And for her children's sake, she had no choice but to accept.

He'd issued his offer as little more than the return of a favor. The type of thing any *friend* would do for another. Chelsa hoped to heaven she could remember that and not let her heart get carried away.

It's all a matter of how you play the game, she told herself.

At last she nodded and stepped back, feeling cold without the warmth of his touch. "It won't take me long to pack."

Chapter Ten

They touched down in the Royal Guard compound and were whisked into Cole's Lincoln with its blacked-out windows that effectively hid the occupant's identities.

"I usually land at the airstrip on the palace grounds," Antonio explained. Sophie was asleep in his lap, her pudgy cheek pressed against his chest, her little lips slightly open. Emily was snuggled in between Chelsa and Raquel, awake and watchful. "Landing at the palace, though, signals the citizens that I am home."

In other words, Chelsa thought, the cloak-and-dagger they were engaging in was to spirit him and Chelsa into the country before anybody knew. Chelsa appreciated the need for stealth, but it reminded her of what was at stake.

That she was very likely hunted.

A weight of dread settled in her stomach as she gazed out the tinted windows.

The car leaned into a turn and the sight before her nearly took her breath. The palace was like something out of a storybook. The driveway must have been at least a half mile long, flanked by exquisite gardens and a magnificent expanse of verdant lawns.

Antonio had told her the structure alone covered seven acres, but she somehow hadn't been prepared for the grandeur of it all, hadn't truly imagined the scope of something that size.

Members of the Royal Guard, looking like life-size toy soldiers in black-and-silver uniforms, stood at attention by the doors and at strategic points around the grounds. Chelsa knew she was gawking, but she couldn't help it.

Sophie was awake now, and both she and Emily were as transfixed as their mother, their noses practically pressed against the Lincoln's tinted window.

"Daunting, is it not?" Raquel said with a smile.

"I can't seem to find the right words."

"You will get used to it soon enough," the heiress said.

That was the problem, Chelsa thought. She *might* get used to it. Dear Lord, had she made the right decision? What about the girls? They'd been uprooted enough lately. Was it fair to allow them to become attached to new people and places, only to tear them away again, to take them back on the run? Because if by some miracle they no longer had to hide, they would eventually have to return to their own home. Leave all this behind.

Leave Antonio behind.

The Lincoln came to a stop and the door opened. Guards formed a stoic aisleway from the car to the front entrance of the palace. Antonio got out, then reached for the girls, lifting them out. Subdued, they each clung to his pants leg, staring in awe at the expressionless guards.

Chelsa gathered up the cat and accepted Antonio's helping hand. She, too, had the urge to cling to his pant leg—or at least his sleeve. The opulence before her was foreign and totally out of her realm.

A fortress against evil.

An insular world of the privileged. Royalty.

Good night, she felt as though she'd stumbled into the middle of a dream. An elusive dream.

He touched her cheek. ''You will be safe here, *querida*. Trust me.''

She nodded and settled the cat into Sophie's outstretched arms. Emily looked a little put out that her sister had beat her out of the honor of carrying Señor Gatito, but kept silent, knowing Chelsa's rule over whoever asked first got their wish, provided they were good about taking turns. Thankfully the cat had traveled amazingly well. Leaving in such a hurry, there'd been no time to search for a pet carrier.

Flanked by Cole and Raquel, Antonio ushered them up the palace steps. The massive oak doors opened into a vast sea of marble, and Chelsa suffered an attack of vanity. Her hair was a mess. With its tendency to frizz, she probably looked like a wild woman. The sea air in San Alegra and the whip of the helicopter rotors had surely added to her disarray.

And when she caught a glimpse of the beautiful woman walking toward them, looking elegant in a buttercup-yellow summer suit, she decided right then that her own twenty-dollar sundress wasn't proper attire.

Especially in the company of a queen!

But thoughts of fashion and protocol and pity parties vanished the instant the excited yap of a dog intruded. The puppy of questionable lineage darted past a man who looked enough like Antonio to be his twin. Prince Joseph, Chelsa realized.

The little dog lost traction against the glassy floor and skidded against the wall, then took off like a shot in the other direction.

Impressions surfaced all at once, too quickly to grab a single one. Señor Gatito, startled by the dog, yowled and leapt from Sophie's arms.

"No, kitty!" Sophie shrieked.

"Sophie!" Emily wailed, automatically assigning blame.

Chelsa didn't have time to referee. Like a scene out of a Keystone Kops comedy, a flurry of voices and activity erupted. Paws clattered and slipped across marble, and a spindly hall table nearly toppled. Dear God, that piece of furniture was probably centuries old! Someone with quick hands grabbed a leaded crystal vase filled with fresh flowers before it tipped. A granite carved statue teetered.

Chelsa might have laughed at the scene if she wasn't so horrified. The hall filled with what looked like the entire royal family, and people were darting to and fro after the animals. Antonio led the pack, looking entirely too gleeful under the circumstances, and Emily and Sophie were hot on his heels, squealing—and running!

Stunned, mortified, Chelsa had trouble finding her voice.

Thankfully the paralysis didn't last more than a beat. "Girls!"

They halted as though they'd smacked into an invisible force field, each looking guiltily over their shoulders.

Even the animals paused.

Antonio snagged the cat. Cole got the mutt.

Princess Briana, holding an infant swaddled in a powder-blue blanket, let out a burst of unrestrained laughter, the exuberant sound echoing off the walls. Her husband, Prince Joseph, stood by, his amused eyes filled with so much love as he gazed at his princess, it almost to hurt to watch.

With the cat under one arm, Antonio grinned, pushed a sexy lock of dark hair out of his eyes and looked at Chelsa.

"Nothing like a mad chase to get the adrenaline pumping." Pointing like a bouncy ball following song lyrics, he said, "Chelsa, meet the family—Joseph, Briana, baby Prince Joseph Lorenzo II and my mother, Isabel. Everybody, this is Chelsa, Emily, Sophie and—" he lifted the cat "—Señor Gatito."

The queen gave a delicate sigh. Tall and regal, with her midnight hair swept into a chic coronet, she stepped forward and extended a hand in greeting.

"My youngest son delights in flaunting convention. Honestly, he was educated by the best in manners—even though it does not show. Welcome to our home. I apologize that my husband is tied up at the moment, but you will meet him when we dine."

Chelsa wasn't sure if she should curtsy or kiss the queen's hand. In the end, she simply shook it politely, still embarrassed over the chaos her arrival had caused.

"I apologize for dropping in on you this way…and for the cat's grand entrance." Dear Lord, not only was her presence putting these royals in danger, now her kids and their adopted pet had likely ruined some priceless treasure. "I'll pay for any damage—"

"Nonsense," Isabel interrupted. "No harm as been

done. And we do not worry about breakage here in the palace, so you must be at ease with your children. Things are made to be touched. How else can one learn and admire? You are welcome here, Chelsa Lawrence.'' She glanced down at the girls. ''As are your precious *niñas* and their pet. As it is, Bri's pup could use a little competition. We have spoiled him terribly. Perhaps another animal will show him he is not king of the palace after all—which will make my husband, Marcos, quite happy.''

''Mother, please,'' Joseph said. ''Irish is sensitive. You mustn't demote him so openly.''

''Irish?'' Chelsa questioned before she could stop herself. Well honestly, the dog was a mutt, with a black ring around one eye and white hair that looked permanently mud stained. A pink tongue lolled out of one side of his mouth in what looked suspiciously like a canine grin. There wasn't a single feature on this mischievous puppy that appeared remotely royal.

''Briana found him in Ireland on our travels last month.''

When Joseph spoke, Sophie turned solemn eyes up to him. ''You don't look like you used to be a frog.''

Chelsa sucked in a breath. Good night, would there be no end to her mortification?

Joseph's brows slammed down and Briana laughed, the sound once again bouncing off the cavernous walls, touching everyone in the vast grand hall.

''Criminy, Joseph,'' Briana said. ''Don't look at the child like that, you'll scare her to death.''

Joseph's expression softened into a look of love so bright, it blinded. It was as though the very walls themselves sighed.

Chelsa wondered what it would be like to have someone look at *her* that way.

She glanced up and saw Antonio watching her. Her heart skittered in her chest. If she went in for fanciful thinking, she might imagine that the soft look he gave her held something more…deeper emotions perhaps.

But that couldn't be. He wasn't the commitment kind.

Joseph knelt before Sophie and tweaked her curly hair. "My apologies, little one. You took me off guard. Do you find my looks appropriate?"

"What's 'propriate?"

"Acceptable, uh…good."

"Yep." She smacked her lips together, and Emily, obviously trying for more decorum than her sister, rolled her eyes. "'Cept water baby frogs are cute, too," Sophie said. "So you could be cute even if you was still a frog."

"Thank you, I think." The prince arched a dark brow, looking from Chelsa to Antonio, seeking clarification.

Antonio grinned. "The water babies are characters in the children's books Chelsa writes."

"Ah, I see." Joseph stood and at last shook his brother's hand, clapping Antonio on the shoulder in affection. "It's good to have you home, Tony. I suspected you would return in time for the Barcelona Grand Prix."

"I've declined to race this season."

A hush fell over the great hall as everyone turned to stare at Antonio as though he'd grown another head…or lost his ever-loving mind. Chelsa wasn't sure what was going on. Especially when they each glanced at her as though she was privy to the secret…or responsible.

Raquel stepped closer to Chelsa and quietly offered clarification. "Tony *never* misses a race or an opportunity for danger."

"Then why is he now?"

Raquel's auburn brows lifted. "If I were a betting woman, I would wager it has something to do with you."

Chelsa wanted to object. They were merely acquaintances; he was a friend offering a haven. He wouldn't change his life-style because of her.

Other than Raquel's softly spoken words and the speculative looks the royal family gave her, the moment passed. They were acting awfully smug, though, as if she'd accomplished some incredible feat.

Briana stepped forward and Raquel cooed over the baby. "Oh, he has grown since I last saw him."

"You saw him yesterday," Bri commented dryly.

"And he has changed," Raquel insisted. "Babies are my business. I should know."

"I suppose you've got another idea for a photograph?"

"Naturally."

Briana laughed. "King Marcos isn't keen on naked pictures of Joseph's royal successor."

"Ah, but Isabel loves them, and we all know who actually rules this kingdom."

The women chuckled and Chelsa watched in speculation. She knew the story of Raquel's betrothal to Joseph. It surprised her that given the history, the two women were so obviously close.

Chelsa had kept her hands folded for as long as she

could, but the urge to reach out and stroke the precious infant's downy cheek got the better of her.

"He's beautiful, Briana."

"Thanks. Would you like to hold him?"

"I'd love to." She accepted the soft bundle, adjusting the blanket to get a better look. Her own babies were too big to be cradled this way. Oh, they cuddled, but there was something about the touch of a baby's sweet hand, the feel of their weight in your arms, the total dependence. It tugged at her heart and clear through to her womb.

Unbidden, she imagined holding Antonio's baby, their baby.

The thought winged out of nowhere, startling her. A dangerous yearning.

She looked up and caught him watching her. His expression was unreadable. He still held the squirming cat. Cole and Joseph had shut the dog in the parlor. The three men were in a discussion. Probably about her.

Antonio broke away from the group and walked toward her.

Feeling as though her thoughts were printed on her forehead, she handed the baby back to Briana, feeling empty and at sea.

What in the world was the matter with her?

Before he could reach her, Emily stopped him.

"Can I take Señor Gatito now?"

"Yes. I believe he will conduct himself in a more befitting manner now that the dog has been banished to the other room."

"Is Irish sad?" Sophie asked.

"Certainly not." He lowered his voice to a conspiring whisper. "There are many wonderful things in the parlor to chew. He is probably having a grand time.''

Briana sucked in a breath, having overheard. ''Criminy! Joseph, get the dog before he finishes off that damask chair!''

Joseph took off like a servant instead of a royal prince.

Antonio laughed, then sobered when the queen shot him a long-suffering look of censure.

''I ought to make you reupholster that chair,'' Isabel said, her smooth features twitching on the verge of a smile.

''Me! It's Joseph's dog. Let him get his royal hands dirty. It'll do him some good.''

''You are an impertinent son. Come, *niñas*,'' Isabel said to Sophie and Emily. ''Let us go to the kitchens and request a dish of milk for your Señor Gatito. Cook has baked wonderful pastries, and we shall be terribly mannerless and snitch a few.''

The kids thought this sounded like a wonderful adventure, and each slipped a hand into the queen's. Cole, Raquel and Briana headed for the parlor to rescue Joseph—or the dog, most likely.

Antonio watched them go, his main attention focused on the queen. His regal mother knew all the dictates of protocol and employed them often enough, but in her home—and around children—she was as soft as a marshmallow.

She was the one woman above all others that he admired.

The palace had been turned upside down by children, an infant, a mutt of questionable lineage and a stray cat, yet his mother took it all in stride as though the grand palace was used to chaotic interludes.

The regal queen was smugly in her element—though she wouldn't admit it openly. And he'd seen that soft look on her face, knew she was already eyeing Chelsa's two little cherubs as potential grandchildren.

A strange shiver went through him. What the hell had possessed him to announce that he wouldn't be racing in the Grand Prix? He'd made the decision without thought. And now the family was writhing with speculation, reading more into the decision than was there, reading more into Chelsa's presence, his bringing her here.

He'd promised himself he'd see Chelsa through her dilemma. That was all there was to it. Nothing deeper.

So why had his heart turned over when he'd looked up and seen her with Briana's son in her arms? Why had he immediately flashed on an image of her holding *his* baby? The thought had stunned him right down to his toes. He'd *never* courted fatherhood. He liked kids, was more than happy to play with them, admire them. But the responsibility of having some of his own and being tied down? Never.

Another niggling thought popped up as his mother and Chelsa's children disappeared around the corner. What was that line about never say never?

¡Dios! He was getting entirely too introspective.

He looked back at Chelsa, noticing that she looked uneasy now that her children were out of her sight.

"My mother will take good care of them. You will have no worries while at the palace. The grounds as well as the interior are monitored twenty-four hours a day. You and the girls will be safe to move about—even outdoors—whenever you like."

"I wasn't worrying. I was thinking how surprised

I am by your family. I expected more formality—present company excepted,'' she said with an impish grin. ''They're all so…so down-to-earth.''

''It has not always been this way. Joseph's marriage to Briana has created the biggest changes. She is forever insisting that she wouldn't know how to be fancy if she tried.''

''I like her. She's very warm, easy. Everyone here is.''

''Ah, but you have not met my father.'' He grinned when her eyes widened. ''Do not look so terrified. There is another area where Bri's presence has engendered change. She has brought joy and laughter into Joseph's life, and her exuberant personality has infused the palace with a casualness that is refreshing. The journalist loves to write about the American princess and her fairy-tale marriage.'' The minute he said the words, he regretted them. Shadows returned to Chelsa's lake-blue eyes.

''I shouldn't have let you talk me into coming here. Sooner or later the media will speculate on who I am.''

He put his hand on her shoulder, kneaded the tense muscles. ''Don't do this, *querida*.''

She shook her head. ''I don't belong here. The skeletons are bound to come out of my closet. As much as you tell me otherwise, it's only a matter of time before they learn my name. Cole said there were people here in Valldoria who were also fleeced by Rick. What if it causes some sort of mutiny or something? Your house'll get egged—''

''Chelsa.''

''The kids will be shunned and not understand why—''

"Chelsa."

"I can't pay them back, even if I wanted to. I don't know who or how much, or—"

He stopped her rambling in the surest way he knew. With his lips against hers. He felt her surprise, her absolute stillness, then her softening. This is what he wanted, her surrender.

Wanted it bad.

But they were in the middle of the grand hallway. Granted, everyone had dispersed, but the moment of privacy wouldn't last.

And he'd created enough speculation as it was.

He eased the pressure of his lips, contented himself with a soft kiss against her brow, then stepped back.

Her eyes were heavy, stunned, her mouth open. It took every bit of his control not to taste again.

Like the shadow of the sun passing before a cloud, her eyes cleared, filled with questions. Her gazed darted around the foyer, a hint of embarrassment there.

Then she smiled sheepishly. "Well, I guess I got a little melodramatic."

He grinned. "A little. But on you it sits beautifully."

She snorted and shoved her riotous curls off her face. "Flatterer. If I promise to exercise some dignity, will you give me a tour of the house?"

"Certainly. However, I will forgive you a lapse in dignity when we tour the sleeping quarters. In fact—"

"Antonio," she warned.

"I cannot help it. I have a reputation to uphold."

She whacked him on the arm. "I think that reputation you hide behind is a big sham."

Something inside him clicked and gave way. He

couldn't put a name to it, but the experience was happening way too often for his playboy, carefree peace of mind.

Still, he could no more stop his next words than he could stop the tide of the sea. He tipped her chin up, held her gaze. "Reputation aside, I want you, Chelsa Lawrence."

Her chest rose on an indrawn breath, making him ache to lower his hand a bit, to touch her there. Beneath the thin cotton, she was naked from the waist up. He wondered if this woman even owned a bra. And hoped to God she didn't.

He saw the fine tremor in her hands as she clasped them together and stepped back, looking everywhere but at him.

"Did…uh, did you say there's two hundred rooms here?"

"Two hundred and forty-four at last count."

"Maybe we could stick with the ground floor and leave the, uh, the bedrooms for another time."

Her flustered stammering charmed him. Hell, everything about this woman charmed him. "Cluck, cluck."

Her shoulders squared. "I am not a chicken. I just have better sense than to get tangled up with the likes of you."

"Ah, *bella,* you wound me." Dramatically, he placed a hand over his heart. There was no insult behind her words. She was merely stalling. And they both knew it.

They both knew that the chemistry between them was growing too strong to be ignored.

"Now look who's getting melodramatic. Move it,

Prince, and don't spare the details. I like a little history mixed in with my tour.''

He urged her forward. "Now I am feeling the light of challenge. Although history was never my strong suit, I should not like you to find me lacking as a guide.''

When her gazed slammed into his, he knew her thoughts were right along with his, picturing images of an entirely different guidance. A sensual guidance.

She'd had a good point. It would be best all around to leave the bedrooms for another day. He had plenty of control. But a man could only take so much.

And the ache in his body told him he was perilously close to the edge.

IT WAS CLOSE to midnight before Antonio escorted her to the guest room she'd be sleeping in. She'd started to argue that the girls should be sharing a room with her, but the queen had adamantly overruled the suggestions. Emily and Sophie were given the choice of their own separate rooms, or bunking together. They had chosen to be together—because neither was willing to compromise on who got to sleep with Señor Gatito.

Chelsa worried that the residents of the palace would get little sleep, though, because Sophie had sneaked Irish into the room with them. Although the puppy and the cat had declared a wary truce, visions of chaos remained in Chelsa's mind.

Antonio moved into the room and opened the leaded glass doors that led to the balcony. Watching the shift of his muscles beneath his shirt was causing havoc with Chelsa's hormones.

They were suddenly alone, and all she could think

about was what had nearly happened last night—before Emily's nightmare had interrupted them.

And even throughout the whirlwind trip to Valldoria, meeting the royal family, touring the palace and dining in the elegant gold room, desire still shimmered. Every time she looked at Antonio, brushed up against him, heard the silky cadence of his Latin accent, a fire ignited in her belly and spread like an out-of-control blaze.

She was hot with anticipation and didn't quite know what to do with it. Needing to cool off, she stepped out onto the balcony.

The evening breeze smelled sweet, the scent of garden flowers wafting in on the air currents. A full moon rode high in the sky, its glow stealing the sparkle of the stars. Colored lights illuminated the magnificent fountains and water gardens, their myriad hues bathing the palace's stone walls, making it look like a true fairy-tale castle.

"Is the room to your liking?"

She smiled. "It's beautiful. I could get spoiled."

He touched her cheek, sending her heart tripping. *"Bueno,"* he said softly, gently. "You deserve to be spoiled."

She looked away, gazing at the lights of the city far in the distance.

"What is it, *querida?"*

"I can't help wondering how many families out there were taken in by Rick." Her hand gripped the iron railing. "What if they find out who I am and picket the palace or something?"

"They would do no such thing. And you are not responsible for your ex-husband's misdeeds."

"More than misdeeds." She shrugged and crossed

her arms, the breeze chilling her bare shoulders. "And I *feel* responsible."

"That is because you are so good...so genuine." He turned her to face him, his hands warm as he rubbed her chilled arms. *"Magnifico."*

He searched her features as though she were a puzzle. Gentle light spilled from the open bedroom door as elaborate fountains two stories below rained spouts of water, making her think of romance, making her imagine they were the only two people in the midst of a beautifully enchanted garden.

A private paradise where dreams were unlimited.

His brown eyes were impossibly dark, intense, hot enough to take the chill out of the night air. She moistened her lips, feeling the desperate tug of desire, aching to test the dimple in his cheek that remained permanent even when he wasn't smiling.

His gaze dropped to her mouth and her breath lodged in her throat, held there suspended on the wings of acute anticipation.

"What is it about you, I wonder." His lips caressed her brow. "One look and I feel I must taste." A whisper across her lips. "Touch."

Her heart tried to beat its way out of her chest. This had been brewing between them from the first moment he'd opened his eyes after the shipwreck. And oh, it felt wonderful. *He* felt wonderful.

"We shouldn't." The words were said against his lips, swallowed by his breath. Even still, her hands slipped from his chest, behind his neck, urging, asking, contradicting.

"But we must," he said in a voice that was raw with need, a need that matched her own.

It was time, she decided. Her love for this man was

bittersweet—like so many other things in her life lately. Nothing could come of it.

But for once, for just a little while, she wanted to set aside all thoughts of danger and responsibility, to shut out the world and take something for herself.

Just for herself.

Here, within the guarded palace walls, within the arms of this very special prince, she was safe. And safety went a long way in allowing desire to blossom.

She would look at it like a fairy tale, a moment out of time in a magical place, in a magical world, with an extraordinarily magical man.

Just once, she promised herself. Just once she wanted to be swept away. She wanted to *feel*. And this man simply made her come alive.

"Yes," she said. "We must."

Chapter Eleven

And indeed she was swept away. The whispered words were barely out of her mouth before he lifted her into his arms and strode into the bedroom, kicking the double doors closed as he went.

A first, Chelsa thought, dazed. No man had ever carried her to bed. It thrilled her, made her giddy. And he accomplished it all without ever breaking contact with her lips.

His innate expertise reminded her of who he was—a reputed Latin lover. Good night, could she measure up?

"You are having second thoughts?" He paused beside the bed and gently lowered her to her feet. Sensuality radiated like a palpable entity as he looked down at her.

She should have known a man like Antonio would be utterly attuned to a woman's every nuance. She shook her head.

"Then what is it, *querida?*"

"I'm no virgin, but I'm feeling a lack of experience here." She tried for a carefree laugh and failed miserably. "Actually, I'm scared silly."

"As am I."

The quiet admission stunned her right down to her toes. She searched his features, looking for signs that he was placating her, trying to ease her fears with a lie.

There were none.

Like a hypnotic suggestion, her muscles relaxed, her mind opened. Her senses came alive as she reached out and unfastened the buttons of his shirt, touched the dark hair that covered his chest. The skin beneath was firm and nicely muscled, testament to his physical life-style. He was a man who lived on the edge of danger.

And that's exactly how she felt right now. On the edge of danger, stepping into the unknown. But a bayou filled with alligators couldn't have stopped her.

Antonio stood still as Chelsa's hands explored him, tentatively at first, then with anticipation and unfeigned pleasure. Her utter concentration tested his control.

He'd had women intent on tearing his clothes off and engaging in hot sex, but even with the most avid, the underlying expectation was still there—that *he* be the one to perform, to show them a good time. It was a part of his life he'd accepted, expected, rarely giving it much thought.

Now here was this tiny woman, a mother of two, wounded emotionally, yet with a core of steel, openly displaying the pleasure she found in simply touching him.

The flush of sensuality on her cheeks and the heaviness of desire in her blue eyes radiated an honesty and genuineness that humbled him. It lent weight to their intimacy, made it important, engaged him in a way he hadn't felt before.

This wasn't recreational sex. This was something more…more than curiosity and satisfaction. And even though that revelation scared him, it made him determined to make it right, to give her as much pleasure as was in his capacity to give. Not because his touted reputation dictated it, but because he wanted to, *needed* to with a desperation that bordered on pain.

His hands wrapped around her hip bones, drawing her body flush against his, letting her feel the strength of his arousal, his urgency. When she sucked in a breath, he nearly lost his tenuous hold on control.

Although she was a woman who had ''commitment'' stamped all over her, he told himself he wasn't playing with her heart, that making love with her would be special, beautiful and would not bring about hurt.

Still his conscience reared—his sense of fair play. She'd suffered enough hurt in her life. He would cut off his arm before he'd add to it.

''I find I must exercise some gallantry, *querida.*''

''Oh, please don't.''

He nearly smiled at the entreaty in her voice. ''I am a flighty sort…not a good bet sometimes. Are you certain this is what you want?''

Chelsa felt an instant stinging around her heart, but the racing desire washed it away, soothed. He was telling her she couldn't keep him, couldn't hold him beyond the moment.

Bittersweet love, she thought again. But this was the fairy tale, the fantasy, and she was going into it with her eyes wide open.

''I'm sure. You're not taking anything that I don't want to give.''

His eyes closed, his brow resting against hers. "Thank you."

Out of nowhere, a bubble of mirth surfaced. "Give it a few minutes before you thank me."

He jerked, his dark brows slamming down at her laughter, especially in the midst of the seriousness. Then his smile blossomed, his teeth startling white against the darker hue of his skin.

"Shame on you, *querida*. It will take me *much* longer than a few minutes to make love to you."

"Big talk," she taunted, glad that the touchy moment had passed.

He made a playful growl deep in his throat. "You would challenge me, *bella?*"

"Us," she whispered. "I want you, Tony."

He cupped her face, threaded his fingers through her wildly curly blond hair. He was shaking. So much for playboy confidence. He'd blown it the moment he'd laid eyes on this woman.

And that was something he was determined to remedy. Chelsa Lawrence was a woman made to be pleasured. He would make this a night to remember, give her all he had to give.

His mouth settled over hers, coaxing, asking for surrender.

Chelsa could have told him she'd surrendered long ago. But she let him lead. "Should we turn out the lights?" she asked against his lips.

"No. I want to see you. I do not want to miss any part of you."

"But the windows—"

"We are three stories up. The position of the bed makes seeing in impossible."

All thoughts of anyone spying on them fled as his

lips traced her jaw, her neck, the ultrasensitive spot just behind her ear.

He eased the strap of her dress off her shoulder, pushed the material to her waist.

"Scandalous," he breathed against her mouth. "Do you have any idea what it does to me to know that you are bare beneath these dresses?"

"Not totally bare," she managed to say. "It's too humid to wear many clothes."

"Thank God for uncomfortable weather."

He eased her onto the bed, and slowly peeled the dress from her body until she lay there before him, wearing nothing but her panties—a mere swathe of ice-blue lace. Holding her only with his gaze, he undressed, then stood in the pool of lamplight, allowing her to look.

And oh, she looked. Fully clothed, he excited her, thrilled her, ignited her fantasies. Undressed, he was simply magnificent.

His gaze was so exclusive, like the softest caress, making her feel cherished, beautiful. She'd never been the total focus of a man's desire before—not in this way—and the experience was so incredible, she couldn't put it in words.

The mattress dipped as he lowered himself beside her. She reached for him, but he stopped her.

"Relax. Enjoy."

"I enjoy by participating." Where in the world had that come from? She saw his eyes darken, saw a muscle twitch in his jaw. Spurred by his response, she set aside any inhibitions and gave him total honesty. "I've never wanted to touch so badly."

"Ah, *bella,* you could easily make me lose control."

"Would that be so bad?"

"No. Not bad. But I have many fantasies I wish to explore, to satisfy. And I am thinking it will take all night."

"All night?" Dazed by the sensual promise, she simply stared, her heart pounding a cadence that left her dizzy.

"Absolutely. Indulge me, sweet Chelsa."

She was helpless to do anything less when his lips and hands moved over her. He caressed her, kissed her so softly. Touched her in just the right places, anticipated her needs before she even knew what those needs were.

Cherished. That was the only word she could come up with. Slowly. Thoroughly. Gently. He savored every inch of her body as though tasting an elegantly prepared dish, taking his time.

She'd half expected a bad boy of the Latin world—rough and arrogant and determined. She learned that he couldn't be pigeonholed. He gave her the best of both worlds. Yes, there was arrogance, a bold sureness that came with sexual self-confidence. But there was also a tenderness, a reverence that made her want to weep.

His lips cruised over her breasts, worshiping, while his palm slid low on her belly. White-hot need scorched through her veins, pumping her heart into a frenzy, muddling coherent thoughts. He found points of pleasure she never knew existed, the underside of her breast, her wrist, the inside of her knee.

Perspiration slicked her skin. Her lungs hurt, felt near to bursting, yet every time she reached for him, tried to hurry, he evaded.

His lips were firm, slipping over her like rivulets

of cool spring rain one moment, then scorching like licking flames the next. Hot and cold. Fire and ice. The contrasting roller coaster of images kept her off balance and at a fever pitch of mind-numbing desire.

The brush of his hair against her inner thigh sent her hips bucking. And when his mouth pressed against the very core of her, she thought she might actually faint.

She couldn't get enough, was certain it was too much. A kaleidoscope of colors burst behind her closed lids. She wanted to scream, to beg.

"Please..." She gripped his shoulders, urging.

"Not yet."

"No," she sobbed, frustration so keen yet so utterly exquisite. "I can't take—"

"Yes. There is so much more."

More? Dear heaven, he'd taken her right to the edge of madness and over the top. She could not conceive of there being more.

But he was true to his word, allowing her only a mere moment of respite before taking her right back up where she teetered perilously close to the peak. It was a skill, pure and simple.

And it made her wild.

Wild to make *him* feel this electrifying tempest, to make him lose that rigid, exquisitely thrilling control, to test her feminine power. This was her fantasy night, her moment out of time. She didn't want to wake up some morning with regrets—regrets that she hadn't experienced all there was to experience with this fascinating prince whom she would love from afar.

And it wasn't fair that he was doing all the giving and she was not giving back as much in return. Regardless of what he'd said, she wanted more participation, needed it, needed to appease as well as be appeased.

Surprising him with her agility, she slipped from beneath his weight, settled on top of him and waged her own brand of sensual war on his body.

Antonio was stunned into immobility for the space of two heartbeats. His hands fisted against the sheets as her lips sketched his torso in quick, clever nips. His first instinct was to demand control back, but her intoxicating, single-minded exploration blanked his mind and held him in the grip of a strange and fascinating paralysis.

Silky strands of hair tickled his thighs. Warm breath teased him. Fire, flashing and incendiary, swept him as her lips and mouth closed over him. For a mind-numbing instant, he thought he'd been transported to another planet, another world, a world of heat and desire and sweet, sweet sin.

She gave so unselfishly, as she did with every other aspect of her life. He felt as though this were his first time. He hadn't realized he'd been jaded about sex. Chelsa taught him he had. No woman had ever given so much, so generously, so willingly.

His brain went numb, blanked for several heartbeats. Urgency built. The unique smell of citrus that was Chelsa's alone, teased him as her lips and hands tormented him. Forgetting to temper his strength, forgetting his suave moves, he gripped her, rolled her over onto her back and swept her beneath him.

"Oh." The word ended on a surprised moan.

He couldn't seem to get enough of her touch, her taste. She made him crazy; she made him feel all male and ten feet tall.

Chelsa was sure she'd died and gone to heaven,

and for the life of her, she couldn't think of why she deserved such an honor. All she could do was feel, yet the feelings were so exquisitely overpowering, she couldn't define any one singly. He turned her mindless, made her forget everything but the two of them, what they were doing, all heat and sensation.

Her legs wrapped around him and her nails dug into his back. She might have been shocked at her avidness, but there was no room for shock. Only for sensation. Sweet, fiery sensation.

And she wanted more.

Wanted it now.

"Please." If he teased her any more, made her wait, she surely wouldn't survive.

He seemed to understand, appeared as lost in the moment as she was.

She felt him press against her, and suddenly she needed to look at him, to watch him, to feel again that exclusiveness, the utter intimacy he telegraphed with a mere gaze.

She cupped his face, looked into his eyes. With gazes locked, he entered her, slowly, sensually, exquisitely.

It was the most erotic thing she'd ever experienced.

The feelings that washed through her at that moment were indescribable. There was love, yes, but there was something more, something she was almost afraid to name.

For several moments he was still, filling her, watching her. His dark eyes were intense, studying her, yet she couldn't read his emotion.

Then the urgency built, like a wave gathering momentum, liquid and powerful, rushing headlong, unstoppable.

Her breathing came faster now, harder. He captured the meager oxygen with his mouth, swept her into a frenzy with his tongue, with the increased tempo of his thrusts.

She wanted the sensations to last forever, but it was impossible. She couldn't fight it. A starburst of brilliant color filled her vision, blinding her. Her body clenched and throbbed, and climaxed in a flash of molten glory.

An unadulterated, unladylike scream was swallowed as his mouth captured hers. His own moan vibrated through her as his body pulsed and his pleasure peaked, sending Chelsa to another glorious plateau— a plateau she didn't think she'd ever recover from, nor would she forget.

"MERCY," CHELSA SAID said when she was sure her voice would work.

He eased to his side and gathered her close, his fingers idly stroking her damp skin. "Ditto."

She smiled against his chest. "Your reputation isn't overrated." She felt him stiffen, and raised up enough to glance at him. She could have sworn she saw a flash of pain in his eyes, an emotion that was quickly masked.

His dimples winked and his voice was low and sexy. "You're welcome, *querida.*"

For some reason she got the impression she'd hurt him, but she didn't know how, and decided not to pursue it. If he was going to take this moment lightly, so would she.

She plunked a quick kiss on his shoulder and settled back in his arms. "Isn't this the point where you reciprocate with proper gratitude?" She couldn't believe she'd said those words. In trying to keep it light she'd blurted the first thing that came to mind. She was horrified. She'd never in her life asked for a performance rating. And from a prince! Albeit a spare one. "Forget I asked that."

"No. I do not believe I will ever forget what we have just shared." His words were utterly sincere, not a trite, standard line.

And that's when she understood the sensitivity beneath the guise of his sexy grin. Antonio was written about in all the gossip columns as a Casanova, a lady's man, a Latin Lover. Women would be drawn to those images, vying for his attention, hoping to be the one to tame him, to taste the forbidden fruit.

Just as she had been.

She tried to tell herself her situation was different, that she was driven by love. But although he might appear devil-may-care, Antonio was a smart man. He knew he was a challenge to women, a trophy at times.

And by her words, she'd reduced their lovemaking to the same terms. Like scores of other women, she'd fantasized about his touch, his technique. She'd made love with him knowing they had no future.

In essence, her actions could be construed as treating him as a piece of meat, a sexy, savvy, wealthy stud.

And the admission made her feel just terrible.

Not knowing how or what to say, she pressed her lips to his neck, wrapped her arms around his chest, let her heart and body speak silently for her. She held him as though he would disappear before her eyes if she let go.

She held him as though she loved him. And because she did, because she could never tell him, her eyes stung.

"Ah, *querida,* you are safe." He returned her fierce embrace, misunderstanding.

It was just as well. "I know," she whispered past the lump in her throat. "If I let go, though, the world will intrude."

"Not for a while longer." He stroked her hair, pressed his lips to her temple.

The tenderness nearly undid her. Before she embarrassed herself and fell apart, she changed the subject. "Tell me about your childhood. What it was like growing up in a palace?"

"Probably not all that different from any other childhood."

"Now, *that* I don't believe."

He chuckled, the sound rumbling in his chest, vibrating in her own. "Well, we *were* expected to conduct ourselves with royal manners—at least in public."

"But you didn't?"

"Rarely."

"Why?"

He shrugged and shifted up in the bed, leaning against the ornately carved, mahogany headboard, resettling her along his side. "I do not spend time analyzing my motives, past or present, but…let me think." His fingers idly trailed over her arm.

"Mother was regal, but she wanted Joseph and I to be as normal as possible. Joseph got more attention from the media and the people because by order of birth, he was next in line for king after my father."

"Did that bother you?"

"I wasn't jealous of him, if that's what you mean.

But…as a child, I did want attention. Childish, I suppose.''

"No," she interrupted. "Normal."

He smiled. Trust her to understand. She was great with kids, even wrote for them. "Anyway, I had a tendency to show off, and the more dangerous the stunt, the more attention I drew. But something happened. What started out as attention seeking, turned into genuine pleasure. I loved danger, loved walking that fine line on the edge, loved the heady surge of adrenaline. I began to live for each new thrill.''

"Just listening to the gleeful tone of your voice makes me glad I have girls. I don't think I'd survive the stuff little boys do."

"Shame on you, *querida*. Girls can live dangerously and do the same thing little boys do."

"Okay, I'll rephrase. I'm glad *my* girls haven't displayed a strong bent toward thrill seeking—and don't you be putting any ideas in their heads." She added strength to her admonishment by giving his chest a light tweak.

"I wouldn't dream of it." His lips curved. He loved watching the animation in her face, loved seeing some of the burdens lifted from her shoulders. He was pleased with the decision to move her to the palace. Here, he could see the woman who wrote fanciful stories, the woman who had a bit of a child in her—like him.

"Now, why don't I believe you?"

"I cannot imagine."

She gave him a mock-stern look, a look that failed completely since she was buck naked. "Continue."

"Where was I…? Ah, yes, thrills." His fingertips stroked the sides of her breasts, and he almost lost the thread of conversation. "Joseph used to tease me that he could refuse his title and force me into doing my royal duty."

"Would that be so bad?"

"Absolutely." He shuddered, adding drama to the movement, even though he grinned. "That is why I am so pleased that he and Briana have a son. Now that lets me off the hook—not that I could ever envision anything happening to my brother which would prevent him from fulfilling his duty. Now, however, for certain my life is my own to live as I like."

"Within reason, surely. Aren't there still expectations from you?"

"Some. But not nearly as many as Joseph has to adhere to."

"Obviously he doesn't mind his position."

"No. However, there was a bit of touch-and-go when he balked at marrying Raquel and ran off to France. He insisted on traveling without bodyguards, and I for one was hasty to remedy this breach on his part."

Chelsa laughed at the drama of his words. "Why don't you have the same entitlements as your brother? Why don't you have bodyguards?" She could have sworn his chest puffed up, could have sworn she could see a burst of testosterone rush through his veins. Which was impossible. But the impression was there nonetheless.

"I am more than capable of looking out for myself, and happy at it. Besides, I am always on the move. Being watched twenty-four hours of the day would be too confining for me."

And just that quickly, she was reminded of the man he was. Gentle, to be sure, loyal, loving. But he wasn't hers to hold. He wasn't anyone's to hold. He was a rolling stone, happy with his life. He wouldn't be confined.

For a few hours, she'd forgotten about their differences, allowed herself to fantasize, to dream. And she'd started this interlude with just that thought in mind. To experience the moment, to embrace the magic of the evening.

But the evening was over. Yesterday had slipped into the wee hours of tomorrow.

And with the dawning of a new day came reality.

She eased out of his arms. "Speaking of being watched, you should probably go." It felt weird telling him what to do in his family's home, but she didn't know any other way to say it.

"Why?"

"Because it wouldn't look right if you're caught leaving my room. I'm a guest here, and I'm starting to feel disrespectful for acting this way under your parents' roof."

"We are in a separate wing, Chelsa. Technically you are under *my* portion of the roof."

"You know what I mean. Maybe your family's used to you having overnight slumber parties with women, but...I don't think I'm sophisticated enough to pull off that sort of confrontation, or—"

"Stop right there." His voice was soft yet tense. "I have never brought a woman to the palace before, never slept with one here. And if you recall, it was my mother who assigned you to my wing of the house."

"Oh."

Antonio watched the color wash over her face. His own words rang in his mind, giving him something to think about. His mother had made no secret of the fact that she'd like to see him settled. Nerves crowded in, making him uneasy. Not the unease of regret. But strange nonetheless. Emotions he wasn't about to analyze too deeply.

He was attracted to Chelsa Lawrence, more than he'd ever thought he could be to a woman. But settled? He wouldn't know the first thing about being settled.

"However, you are probably right. We would not want the *niñas* to burst in and get the wrong impression."

He stood and pulled on his pants, then bent to give her a soft kiss. Her lips clung. A warning sounded in his brain.

Dios, had he told her he wasn't the settling-down kind? Yes, he was positive of it. Had she forgotten? Built sand-castle dreams anyway? Aw, hell. He had a firm rule about hurting woman. And this one in particular he would never want to hurt.

He eased back, a mere breath, looked into her eyes.

She smiled and cupped his cheek. "Night, Tony."

He hesitated. Easy words. Dismissing words. Now he was the one reluctant to leave. He was the one who wanted to cling.

¡Madre de Dios! He was the one building the fantasy castles.

Chapter Twelve

Antonio wanted to look in on Chelsa, but it was still early by most people's standards, so he went in search of someone he knew was a morning person. Besides, for the first time in his life he felt uncomfortable, not knowing quite how to handle the typical morning after.

¡Dios! That was not an admission he would care to have leaked.

As he'd suspected, Joseph was already in his office in the west wing, hard at work.

"Just seeing you slaving over this desk makes me glad I am the second born."

Joseph looked up, cocked a brow and nodded toward a crimson leather chair. "Come in. Do what you do best—watch other people work."

Antonio grinned and sat, not taking offense. He and his brother often traded friendly insults. "And here I thought Briana would have cured you of snippiness by now. I shall have to speak to her."

"Give me a break. I've got to keep my edge somehow, otherwise my negotiating power is nil. Now that you are here, I can get some much-needed practice."

"As long as your princess isn't within earshot?"

Joseph grinned.

"You've got it bad, *mi hermano*. Feel free to snarl at will."

"I knew there was a reason I liked having you around. Speaking of lady loves, I like yours."

"She's not—"

"Your usual style?" Joseph interrupted. "I agree. Although I'm not happy about her bad circumstances with the ex-husband, I must admit, I'm glad she's here. I have always wanted a ringside seat to watch your fall."

Antonio tried for a casual tone even though his insides were jumping as though he were facing a guardrail with the accelerator stuck. "I am *not* falling. And Chelsa's *not* my lady. I am merely doing a good deed."

"Is canceling your entry in the Barcelona Grand Prix also part of the good deed?"

"Why is everyone making so much of that? Can a man not change his mind?"

"Most men, yes. You are a different breed."

"I said you could snarl—not malign my character. If Joseph II was not so small yet, I might challenge you to a duel. However, since I am confident that my combat skills are far superior to yours, I will restrain myself." He folded his arms across his chest and slouched in the chair. "I would not want the consequences of responsibility. I am much too happy being the spare."

"Careful, little brother. I might issue a challenge of my own. It would do you good to accept a few of the royal responsibilities."

Antonio grinned, thankful that he'd accomplished his initiative—to steer the conversation away from the touchy subject of him and Chelsa. And they both knew Antonio did plenty with regard to upholding royal commitments—just not to the extent that was required of Joseph.

"Alas, if you continue to threaten my person with violence, I will be very tempted to tell Mother."

Joseph snorted—very unprincelike. "The day you tell on me to the queen is the day I'll eat my royal ribbons."

Laughing, Antonio picked up a Baccarat paperweight, and without a care for its outrageous value, tossed it from hand to hand like a tennis ball. "At least I am back in that woman's good graces."

"Yes," Joseph agreed. "By butting into both mine and Raquel's lives."

"And aren't you glad that I did?" He rubbed the crystal against his shirt as though shining an apple. "Rocky is happy as a clam with Cole, and you, my brother, are glowing like a Christmas tree. I have always though it was fairly ridiculous to expect me to hand out advice to the lovelorn, but obviously I am better at it than I had thought."

"Perhaps you have been taking some of your own advice? Seems there's an extra glow about you, too."

Aw, hell. Now they were back to the subject he didn't want to explore. "If I am glowing, it is merely because the queen is not scowling at me. And I would like to keep it that way, thank you. That is the only reason I insisted Chelsa and her daughters come to the palace. I did not want to take the chance of falling *out* of favor once more in the event danger befell the Lawrences on Castillo land—the island. *That's* why I brought her here. *Not* because I was bringing her home to meet the folks, as it were."

"Are you trying to convince me or your yourself, brother?"

Antonio felt like he was mired in quicksand and sinking fast. The more he said, the deeper he sank. "Do not read more into the relationship than is there." Just saying the words made him feel odd. Especially in light of what he and Chelsa had shared last night. Earthshaking. Powerful. A first for him.

¡Dios! He needed some air. Needed freedom. He'd made a vow to see Chelsa through her dilemma. That's the reason he wasn't heading for Barcelona right now. Besides, he didn't need the money. A few million here and there wouldn't make a difference. He had more money now than he knew how to spend.

However, a quick burst of reckless speed would do wonders for him, clear the cobwebs out of his mind, perhaps shake this niggling feeling of...of, well, he couldn't quite put his finger on it. Whatever it was, though, it made him nervous.

He stood. "Care to take a spin in the Ferrari?"

"Conversation getting too hot for you?"

"I am used to hot conversations, Your Highness." He deliberately misunderstood, evaded, resorted to sexual innuendo—which was his forte. Or had been. "And do not ask me to tell all. You are a married man now, and you may no longer live vicariously through my adventures." He'd shared stories with his brother before—of women. The thought of sharing his experience of Chelsa, though, was out of the question. It was too private. Too soul stirring.

Unconsciously he rubbed a hand over his heart. "Last chance. Nothing like speeding around in a Ferrari to get the day started right."

"No thanks. You go risk your neck. I've got to protect mine so you don't have to take over."

"Always thinking of me." He tossed the crystal paperweight, grinned when Joseph snagged it. "I appreciate it."

On his way to the garage, Antonio passed through the kitchen, which was bigger than the entire bungalow Chelsa had been staying in on San Alegra.

It was still early, but the staff was hard at work. Marta, wearing a starched apron tied around her ample hips, waved a wooden spoon like a maestro and spoke in rapid Spanish as a platoon of cooks busily prepared pastries and breakfast dishes.

Normally the royal family didn't enter the kitchens—other than the queen when she wanted to direct the staff for celebratory occasions...or more recently, make little girls feel welcome with cookies—but Antonio had never adhered to protocol. Some of his fondest memories were of getting underfoot in this room and of Marta scolding him over his daredevil stunts or for snitching food.

Marta claimed that she was older than dirt and that she would still be ruling these kitchens for generations to come. He believed her. And he was crazy about her.

He slipped up behind her and kissed her cheek. "Hey, beautiful. Have you missed me?" She blushed, distracted, and he reached around her, snagging a piping hot blueberry tart.

Marta didn't miss a thing. She smacked him lightly with her wooden spoon. "Mind your manners, Prince Antonio."

"Ah, Marta, Marta." He shook his head, inching

toward the door. "I am away just a short time and already you forget that I am just the spare."

"Do not talk to me about spares. Now sit, show the manners that your good mother, the queen, has spent money and years to teach you. Have your breakfast like a civilized person."

"Can't. Just passing through."

Her dark red lips pursed. "You are leaving again so soon? But what of the *niñas?* And their sweet *madre?*"

Aw, hell, even the staff were building a relationship where there was none. "I'm not leaving Valldoria," he clarified. "I am only going out for a while."

"Oh. *Bueno.* But do not be long. You must not desert your guests."

The kitchen was feeling awfully hot—just like Joseph's office had. With a hasty wave, he let himself out the side door and walked toward the garage, a detached structure that could house no less that thirty vehicles.

The airplane and helicopter were kept separately in a hangar next to the landing strip, and he fought the restless urge to head that way, to take to the skies and see where he ended up.

But he couldn't. The desire to make sure Chelsa and the kids were safe was even stronger after last night. So he contented himself with the Ferrari.

Pulling the canvas cover off, he ran his hand over the fiery red paint job. It was a sweet piece of machinery. Compact and streamline. He could picture Chelsa beside him, her hair blowing in the wind, a radiant smile on her face.

She was a woman who would appreciate adventure. Right now she had too many responsibilities on her shoulders to let herself enjoy life's simple pleasures, but hopefully that would be over soon.

He could just imagine her joy as he showed her his country, and all it had to offer. Maybe he'd even suggest she drive the Ferrari. He'd bet she'd handle it like a pro. And the kids would get a kick out of seeing their mother let her hair down.

He glanced at the rich leather of the compact interior, and frowned. No back seat to speak of. Maybe he ought to think about buying a family car, something more along the lines of the Rolls or the Mercedes.

The minute the thought surfaced, he slapped a hand to his forehead. Surely he had a fever and it was affecting his brain—or more likely, his heart.

CHELSA WASN'T SURE what was expected of her as a guest, but surely it wasn't staying in bed past eight o'clock! She leapt out of bed and dressed in a hurry, nearly scaring herself to death when she looked in the beveled mirror above the dresser.

Her hair was wilder than usual.

Her stomach gave a funny tickle when she remembered the reason for the disarray, remembered how Antonio had run his hand through it last night, of how they'd practically wrestled in the bed.

And oh, how incredibly good it had been.

Scraping her hair into a ponytail and adding a light blue ribbon that matched the peonies in the print of her dress, she dragged the brocade spread off the floor and made up the bed. Heaven forbid if the maid came in and saw the state of the sheets with their corners untucked.

They'd know for sure what had taken place here.

She took a good look around the room, something she'd been too distracted to do last night. Sun streamed in the windows and glass doors. Plump cushions in restful yellows, golds and whites rested in the window seat, inviting one to curl up with a book and simply watch the world go by. The walls were painted the softest buttery yellow, contrasted with lots of wood and crown moldings painted stark white.

A feeling of peace enfolded her like a soft old quilt, something she hadn't expected—especially here in a royal palace. Or was it that she just felt different after making love with Antonio?

Idly she trailed a finger over a keepsake box made of platinum and glass with a foil-print lid exquisitely rendered in cherubs and hearts. Stunning Waterford and Baccarat crystal vases held huge arrangements of fresh flowers. In addition to the roses and orchids, sachets perfumed the air, reminding her of being in a potpourri shop. She'd never quite managed to get her home to smell this way, no matter how many candles she'd lit or scented oils she'd purchased.

The sound of giggles from the next balcony alerted Chelsa that the girls were up, and she went to their room, where the faint scent of animals vied with the orchid sachet in the suite. She looked around for puppy puddles or signs that the cat had clawed the drapes. No visible disasters were evident.

"Good morning, girls. Did you sleep okay? Any bad dreams?" Guilt zinged her. Would she have even heard her daughter call out?

Emily rolled her eyes as though Chelsa had forgotten a very important lesson. "Antonio said they couldn't come back because they have ears and he told 'em not to.''

"Oh, of course. Silly me.''

"Momma!'' Sophie said. "Irish and Señor Gatito sleeped wif us!''

"In the bed?'' Automatically she checked the sheets, found them unsoiled and pulled up the comforter. She didn't want housekeeping to go to any extra work on their account. Never mind that was their job. Chelsa wasn't used to it. "Did you keep them both here all night?''

"Yep. But they was real good.''

"They didn't need to go outside?'' Dear Lord, she'd been so caught up in her own runaway hormones, she hadn't considered the possibility that the girls might go wandering.

"Marta put newspapers on the porch,'' Emily said. "And a kitty box. Briana said Irish gets accidents sometimes, but that would be okay.''

Chelsa didn't think so. The ornately patterned carpet must have cost the earth. "Well, shall we try to find our way downstairs?''

"Me and Sophie know the way.'' Emily slipped her hand into Chelsa's as though sensing her unease in an unfamiliar place. "Grandmama Isabel showed us all the stairs and rooms. And there's a swimming pool in the house! Right inside, big as you please.'' This was said with a fair amount of awe.

Chelsa was still back a few sentences, though. "Grandmama? Emily, where are your manners?'' Dear heaven, she knew her girls hungered for a father and two sets of grandparents and normality like their little friends, but calling the queen Grandmama was going a bit far. "You should call her Mrs. Castillo, or Queen, uh…'' She'd taught her daughters not to call their elders by their first names. Did that still apply with a queen? She wasn't sure of the protocol. ''Well, I'm sure Grandmama isn't appropriate.''

''But she said we could call her that. She's in training for baby Joseph and we're helping her 'member.'' Dismissing the subject slyly, Emily turned flirty eyes up to Chelsa. ''Can we swim, Momma? Please?''

''We'll see, honey. Right now, though, we ought to see about breakfast.''

''Wait!'' Sophie said. ''Irish gots to go potty first.'' She twisted the knob on the French doors that led to the balcony and carefully herded the animals out. ''No, sweetie-pie,'' she said to the cat. ''You go in the sandbox. Puppy gets the papers. Good puppy.'' She patted the poor dog so hard its back legs nearly gave out. The cat was smarter, steering clear.

Still holding Emily's hand, Chelsa moved to the balcony. Like the one off her room, it looked down on the elaborate gardens and water fountains of the main square. The palace was laid out in a U-shape. Massive gates, too far away to see, were normally open to visitors, but Antonio had assured her that while she was here, the main gates would remain locked and guards would monitor all comings and goings.

Another reminder that she was disrupting their royal lifestyle—possibly putting them all in danger.

''I'm not sure the two of you should be out here on the balcony by yourselves.''

''The king said so, too, and put the kitty box in the bathroom, but it stinked so Sophie and me took it outside.''

''The king?'' Good night. She'd totally fallen down

on her motherly duties. She had no idea who all her kids had interacted with.

And a king handling kitty litter? Oh, dear. "I'm sure everyone appreciates your desire to keep the room clean and sweet smelling, but promise Momma that you won't go outside alone anymore."

She hated that she had to give the reminder. Hated the solemnness that came over the girl's faces. She bent, gathered them both in her arms and kissed them. "I love you both so much. I just want to be able to look at you all the time. Forgive me for being overprotective."

"We love you, too," Emily said.

"I forgive you," Sophie said, though she didn't know for what.

Tears backed up in Chelsa's throat. She cleared them away and stood. "Come on. I'm starving. Let's go eat."

The minute they opened the bedroom door, the animals darted out and a mad race ensued.

"Oh, no, not again." Forgetting her lectures on decorum, Chelsa hiked up the hem of her dress and sprinted down the hall. With a quick word of caution tossed over her shoulder to the girls, she led the way down the sweeping staircase, the three of them sounding like a herd of stampeding elephants.

A maid peeked out a door on the second-floor landing and smiled. Chelsa offered a hasty apology. It wasn't until her feet touched marble that she realized she'd forgotten to put on her shoes. But she didn't have time to agonize over that right now. There were animals to be caught.

She literally slammed into Antonio as she rounded the corner into the dining room.

He chuckled, steadying her. Mortified, she realized the whole family was there. Isabel held the baby, Briana had snagged the puppy and King Marcos held the cat.

Sophie and Emily caught up and bumped into Chelsa, sending her all the way into Antonio's arms.

With the royal family looking on in various degrees of curiosity and speculation, she wished for a nice big hole to open up and swallow her. Her face flamed. Her ponytail was knocked askew. She reached up and tried to fix it. Antonio batted her hands away and pulled out the ribbon, letting her hair fall wildly around her shoulders.

"Good morning, *querida*. I love a woman who makes an impressive entrance."

She actually growled—albeit under her breath. But Antonio heard and laughed. And suddenly Chelsa saw the humor in the scene. She must have looked a sight. Laughter tickled her stomach and throat and she swallowed repeatedly. Gathering her poise and dignity, she turned to the occupants of the room.

"Please forgive me for running in the house." The statement was so absurd. Briana was the first to shout with laugher, and Chelsa simply couldn't hold it in any longer. If it weren't for Antonio's steadying hand, she might have fallen over as her shoulders shook. And the more she thought about it, the harder it was to sober up.

It wasn't until she got a good look at King Marcos's face that she finally found the strength to rein in her mirth.

"Oh, Your Majesty, I do apologize. Here, let me take the cat."

"Sit," he ordered gruffly, stroking Señor Gatito between the ears. Both king and cat looked perfectly content in one another's company—though both were doing an adequate job of pretending otherwise.

Chelsa wasted no time in obeying, determined to restore her dignity. With a practiced look, she silently admonished the girls to mind their manners. She wanted them next to her where she could reach them, but they both streaked around to the other side of the table closest to Briana and the king—and the rowdy animals.

With the practiced eye of a mother who knows her children well, she saw the disaster coming.

Sophie hopped into the chair and nearly pulled the tablecloth off. Joseph's quick hands saved the heirloom china. Emily huffed and nudged her sister—a little too hard—and Sophie fell out of the chair.

The queen refereed, Briana's laughter pealed and Chelsa rested her face in her hands, resisting the urge to peek through her fingers to see what calamity would occur next.

Antonio's hand on her thigh made her jump as though she'd been goosed.

She looked at him, at those sexy dimples and killer smile. "Please tell me your family's suffered disruptions like this before."

His grin widened. "Not many."

She groaned. "I was afraid of that."

Before she could formulate another apology, Raquel swept into the dining room, a camera slung around her neck. It was the strangest thing, Chelsa thought. There was no discomfort or covert looks over the fact that Raquel had been chosen and groomed to be Joseph's princess. Nothing to suggest there'd been intimacies between them, or jealousy on

Briana or Cole's part. Then again, Antonio had mentioned that the heiress and Joseph had rarely spoken.
Well, they all seemed easy enough with one another
now.

And Chelsa had to wonder about her stereotypical
images of just how a princess-in-training was taught.
Looking at Raquel, it was obvious that the rules were
much looser nowadays than she'd imagined—Raquel
was wearing another of those skintight outfits that exposed her middle. Although her pregnancy was in the
very early stages, Chelsa wondered if the heiress
would be the next celebrity to pose for *Vanity Fair*
in all her pregnant splendor. She was gutsy enough.

Cole followed his wife into the room.

The girls, thank heavens, were distracted by the
beautiful newcomer and her adoring husband, and
now sat like picture-perfect china dolls. Pride swelled
in Chelsa's chest.

King Marcos scowled at Cole, then glanced point-
edly at the camera around Raquel's neck. "I thought
we discussed my views on photographs of the young
prince."

"You discussed, dear," Isabel interrupted smoothly.
"We've overruled."

Speechless, he stared at his queen—then gawked
in masculine bewilderment at both Briana and Raquel
when each woman added their comments.

"Joey is a perfect photographic specimen," Briana
said, reaching over to stroke her son who cooed con-
tentedly in his grandmother's arms.

Marcos nearly went into a fit over the prince being
called Joey…and a *specimen*.

"And, Your Highness," Raquel added, snagging a
slice of bacon out the silver service dish on the side-

board, "baby Joe is not the only sweet face in this room. Chelsa's daughters are also on my list—provided I can talk their mother into agreeing." She took a bite of bacon, which apparently didn't agree with her newly pregnant constitution, and set it aside.

The king obviously knew when he was licked. "Now why would anyone in this room think Mrs. Lawrence's opinion would count for anything? My own, as king, does not." He stood and grumbled a parting shot. "I will call a meeting on the merits of men controlling their women."

Antonio prudently held his grin until his father left the room. Then he leaned close to Chelsa. "Do you think he noticed that he took Señor Gatito with him?"

Chelsa pressed her lips together. "Maybe he intends to separate the animals to restore some order."

"Could be."

"I'm surprised at your mother contradicting him in front of the family. I thought that sort of thing was reserved for pillow talk."

"Used to be. Until he tried to force Joseph to marry Raquel. Mother threw a fit, packed her trunks and left."

"She left him?"

"Only for a while. Just long enough to talk sense into Briana."

"Oh. How sweet."

"Don't let her hear you call her sweet. She likes to give the impression she's tough. She does an excellent job, too. Scares me right down to my toes."

"Antonio," Queen Isabel said, pitching her voice to be heard down the vast length of the table. "The rest of us are reluctant to converse for fear of intruding upon your conversation. Would you care for privacy?''

"What an excellent idea, Mother. I was just about to suggest that I show Chelsa around Valldoria.''

"That is a lovely idea. The two of you enjoy yourselves. I will supervise the photographing of the children.''

"Oh, no," Chelsa objected. "I can't impose on you all to baby-sit.''

"Nonsense. You are not imposing when we have offered. There is much beauty to see in our land, but I fear the *niñas* would become bored before you could do your tour justice.''

Antonio watched the expressions flit across Chelsa's face. He'd tossed out the first thing that came to his mind lest his mother's comment about privacy had embarrassed Chelsa. Yet, the more he thought about it, the more he wanted to show her his country.

Privately.

He wanted to watch her expressions, the quick, easy smile that often became stifled beneath her burdens. There were hidden facets to this woman that drew him.

She caught him off guard merely by walking into a room. That wholesome, Earth Mother aura touched him, and he'd simply find himself arrested by the sight of her, distracted.

Charmed.

He couldn't remember any woman having such an effect on him, and he'd squired many—movie stars, models, heiresses, even a Russian princess.

Yet this Southern belle moved him, made his heart beat faster and his stomach turn to mush.

He'd seen the way his father looked at the queen, how Joseph looked at Briana, how Cole couldn't keep his gaze off Raquel. Happy couples, all of them. Content.

It made him envious…and maybe a little uneasy.

It also made him uneasy that his family kept looking at him as though he'd had extensive plastic surgery and they no longer recognized him. So, okay, maybe he *was* a little different, but it was only temporary—just until Chelsa was in the clear and able to live the normal life she deserved.

Yes, a day of sightseeing would be good for them. It would also get them away from the speculative eyes of his family.

He scraped back his chair and stood, gallantly holding out his hand to Chelsa. "What do you say, *bella?* Will you trust me as tour guide?"

"Is it safe?"

Their gazes locked and an emotion he couldn't decipher flickered in her lake-blue eyes. Was she remembering their exercise in trust? Remembering what he'd said about trusting him with her safety but not her heart? Her question could easily apply to both. Especially after last night.

But they still had an audience and he chose to take her question at physical value.

"Just covering the palace grounds will take most of the day, and the perimeter is well guarded. As for the children, with my mother and Briana and Raquel present, they'll be surrounded by an army of bodyguards."

Raquel, overhearing this, thought to object. She glanced at her husband. "Really, Cole. I understand the necessity of guards, but I will need room to work.''

Cole scowled, yet his love was so evident, it ruined the stern expression. ''Don't give me a hard time, Spitfire. You know I haven't yet recovered from you walking right into that kidnapping.''

''I held my own just fine,'' she said smugly.

While the Martinezes engaged in good-natured bickering, Antonio pulled Chelsa to her feet.

''Believe me, they'll be well watched,'' he said.

Chelsa nodded. ''Let me get some shoes.''

This announcement brought everybody's attention to her bare feet.

In the formal dining room.

Face flaming, she hurried out of the room.

Antonio followed, grinning, thoroughly charmed.

Chapter Thirteen

Antonio decided he really did make a dismal tour guide. He was too busy watching Chelsa to point out the sights. At times she would glance at him, and he sensed that she was a little uncomfortable over the intimacy they'd shared last night and didn't quite know what to say or how to act. But the beauty of the estate distracted her—and in turn, Chelsa distracted him.

He found himself unable to look away from her.

A butterfly resting on a dandelion delighted her. The breeze in her hair made her pause. And Antonio was transfixed, afraid to look away lest he miss some new and enchanting expression.

And that's when he knew exactly where he would take her.

Chelsa held her sandals in her hand, preferring to go barefoot, loving the sensual feel of lush cool grass under her feet. They crossed a meadow richly sprouting flowers in golds and lavenders. As they neared a dense stand of trees, the air cooled. The sound of rushing water teased her senses, making her want to explore.

She glanced at Antonio who'd been strangely silent on their walk, his mood thoughtful.

Was he thinking the same thoughts as she was? Nature, in all its glorious splendor was having a field day with her imagination. Two dragonflies connected head to tail sent her memories off on a wild tangent. Bees buzzing around the nectar of flowers and birds calling to their mates all took on sexual connotations in her mind.

Maybe this nature walk wasn't such a good idea after all.

She was about to suggest they turn back when he touched her waist, guiding her past the shelter of trees. Rather than taking note of their surroundings, she glanced at him. Her heart and stomach automatically flipped. All it took was a touch or look and she turned to mush.

He spoke so easily with his eyes alone. Intimately. A tender look that ignited a fire in her belly. So exclusive. With a mere gaze he brought back all the exquisitely thrilling emotions of their lovemaking. Made her yearn.

He paused and pulled her close to his side. "Look," he said softly.

She drew in a breath at the sight before her. The grotto was breathtaking. Waterfalls spilled over huge boulders into a serene lake surrounded by ferns and lush vegetation. It was like something out of a travel brochure, like a painting of a place that couldn't possibly exist.

Yet it did. Paradise.

"Oh, Tony, how can you bear to leave this place? Surely you've never found beauty to duplicate this?"

His fingertips toyed with the hair that brushed her

shoulders. "I thought you'd like it here. Perhaps it will inspire another water baby adventure."

She noticed that he easily sidestepped her comment about staying put in one place. And water babies were the farthest thing from her mind right now. The touch of his fingertips, his dark eyes focused on her so completely, the lock of hair that flopped over his forehead, his overwhelming masculinity—all she could think about was him, of them...together.

Good night, she had sex on the brain. What had gotten into her?

Staring into his deep chocolate eyes, she lost her train of thought. What had he said? Oh, yes, ideas for water babies. "Yes." She had to stop, clear her throat. "Um, it's inspiring."

His hand was toying with the strap of her dress now, easing it off her shoulder then back in place. "Does it inspire anything else?"

Her tongue stuck to the roof of her mouth for several heartbeats. "Like what?" Dumb question. But it wasn't the place so much that inspired fantasies. It was the man.

"Ever gone swimming beneath a waterfall?"

"I didn't bring a suit."

"Ah, *querida,* who needs a suit?"

"I'm not going skinny-dipping with you." What should have come out as a strong statement ended up a weak whisper.

His lips turned up, his dimple creasing. "Why not?"

His gaze swept her, leaving a trail of fire wherever it touched. He was speaking without words again. His eyes said he'd seen everything she had. And that he appreciated it...and would like to see it again.

Touch her again.

And oh, she wanted that, too.

Birds twittered in the trees. Foliage rustled in the gentle breeze. Chelsa's palms began to sweat and the cool rush of water over rocks was having a heyday with her fantasies.

He slipped the strap off her shoulder, pressed his lips to her collarbone, then lower.

And Chelsa was lost. Lost in his touch, in the tender, seductive, exciting man he was.

The fact that they could get caught made the situation more enticing, made her heart beat faster. Dear Lord, where had a thought like that come from? What was the irresistible draw of this man that made her continually want to throw caution to the wind and simply allow herself to be swept away? Made her literally *yearn* to be swept away.

By this man alone.

Okay, subconsciously, was she looking at him like some prehistoric cave woman might...albeit in a nineties way? He was a man who could definitely protect her nest, and provide her every heart's desire—monetarily. Was that the elemental attraction?

His thrill-seeking on the one hand might appear irresponsible, yet the fact that he courted danger—beat it— turned her on. Go figure. Especially for someone like her who prided herself on having her feet firmly planted on the ground.

On the other hand was the life-style. So different from hers. So different than she'd ever even allowed herself to dream. And dangerous. Purposefully dangerous. Seeking that danger even.

In a way he was similar to Rick, gambling on the

come line. But life had a way of crapping out. Eventually the dice would turn cold.

And what of her children then? Her girls had lost one father already. Could she do that to them again? Take a chance and lose? Because the loss wouldn't only affect her. She had an idea that to Emily and Sophie, losing Antonio would be a hundred times more scarring and devastating than losing Rick.

She closed her eyes, hating this particular train of thought. Good night, she had the man poised with one foot in the grave already.

And he was definitely alive.

And making *her* come alive.

Making her unable to resist. No matter what her head said, her heart spoke a different tune.

"You are thinking deep thoughts, I think." His thumb swept over her bottom lip.

"It's a curse."

"Ah, no. A man would be hard-pressed to find faults in you." His fingertips traced the upper swell of her breasts. "You are so beautiful, Chelsa Lawrence." His eyes asked the question. He would go no further without consent.

"Someone might see," she whispered.

"No. We are alone." His lips brushed hers, so lightly.

She rose on tiptoe, clung, wanting more. "I've never done anything like this before."

She felt him grin against her lips. "Ah, *querida,* you wound my ego. You have forgotten last night so soon?"

"I don't mean... I mean, out in the open, in the water."

"Nor have I. Shall we experience a first for both of us?"

Oh, she liked the sound of that. She didn't imagine there were many firsts she could experience with Antonio. He was a man well traveled, well lived.

She took a step back, eased the straps from her shoulders, down her arms, let it skim her torso and pool at her feet.

The arrested look on his face as she stood before him in only a brief pair of lace bikinis gave her the courage to stand proud.

He leaned against a fern-covered boulder as though needing support. "*Dios,* you steal my breath, my thoughts."

He watched her with an intensity that was so strong, almost too strong. She ached, throbbed, felt embarrassed, and shy…and bold.

Turning, she stepped into the water, surprised it didn't sizzle with the way her blood was scorching her veins. Every nerve ending she possessed was screaming at fever pitch as she looked back at him.

Slowly he pushed away from the rock and began unbuttoning his shirt, his eyes never leaving her.

She couldn't look away. He looked sexy and dangerous—she'd never known that the sight of a man undressing could be so erotic.

Her heart pounded when he moved toward her, slowly, proudly, his steps measured and sure, filled with purpose.…

Filled with a single-minded, sensual intensity solely for her. Both a challenge and an invitation.

And more than anything, she wanted to meet that challenge, accept the invitation. Her mouth went dry and she licked her lips. His eyes flared, and his jaw went rigid. His intent fairly shouted, making her tremble. The power of this man scared her...thrilled her.

For endless moments, time seemed to stand still as she waited, watched, anticipated. Water rippled and lapped at her breasts as he came closer, reached for her, and brought her into his arms.

Exactly where she wanted to be. Where she wanted to stay.

His lips caressed, sipped, teased. He seemed to sense the strength of her need, and without question or apology his thigh pressed between hers, making her burn, making her ache in new and wonderful ways.

Water spilled off a shelf of rocks, pouring into the lake like a sheet of glassy silk. She hardly noticed when it rained over her head, soaking her hair, because Antonio was right there to sip the moisture from her skin, from her face, from the tips of her breasts, feasting as though it was the sweetest nectar and he was a man dying of thirst.

Her nipples were pebble hard, pressing against his chest. His tongue did clever things to her ear, her neck, raising chills along her flesh. Water swirled and caressed, heightening the incredible sensuality. She moaned when he eased her panties down her legs, feeling free, open, decadent and filled with urgent need.

She pressed against him, aching, needing to assuage the ache. It felt as though a scream were building in her chest, something powerful that needed an outlet. She wrapped her legs around his waist and clung.

If there was one thing she'd learned in the past year

it was that nothing was for certain. Her time with Antonio was uncertain.

The silent scream turned to a lump in her throat.

"Make love to me, Tony." *Love, not sex. Let me pretend.*

"Ah, *bella,* I am." His accented voice was gravelly with a need that matched her own. Yet he paused, searched her features as though he were reading her thoughts.

She closed her eyes, not wanting him to see the strength of her emotions. Her love. She wouldn't do that to him.

The feel of his touch changed subtly, became exquisitely gentle, impossibly reverent, as though he understood the importance of the moment. Tenderly, thoroughly, in silence, he fitted their bodies together and entered her, taking her on a journey of passion so sweet, so exciting, there was no room for words or thought.

Cocooned between the sheet of cascading water and the rock wall of the grotto, he made love to her as though she were made of the most precious, fragile glass. His deep brown eyes held a tender, quiet sense of understanding, as if he'd looked into her soul and seen every secret, every triumph and every failure.

And in this special Eden, with the cool splash of water surrounding them, he unearthed the secrets, celebrated the triumphs, kissed away the hurt and shame of failures, gave her hope.

He gave her the gift of himself with a sensual poignancy that moved her to tears.

SOMETHING HAD CHANGED between them, but Chelsa couldn't quite put her finger on what it was. There was a silent reserve to Antonio as they walked back to the palace, a silence that held a profound quality. It made her uneasy, uncertain, and yet it made her hope.

Maybe there could be a chance for them after all. She glanced at him, the lack of conversation stretching her nerves. Would it be so wrong to probe a little, to see if he'd open up? She decided to give it a chance.

"I can't believe we did that out in the open and—" They'd made it as far as the grand hall before she looked down. "Oh, my gosh! The front of your pants is all wet!"

The gentle amusement in his eyes accompanied the deep dimple in his cheek. "I did not want to leave your sexy panties floating in the lake for the ducks to drag about."

"So you put them in your pocket? Antonio—" She stopped when she heard a familiar voice coming from the parlor.

A man's voice with a slow, lazy, Mississippi drawl.

Her heart gave a deep thud, bringing her crashing down to reality. Stolen moments in paradise were at an end.

"I think it's best if we don't tell Chelsa."

That comment sent her blood rushing. Without regard for privacy, not even bothering to knock, she stepped into the room. "Tell Chelsa what?"

Cole, Joseph and Detective Mitch D'Ambra whipped around in unison. All three men appeared to have been struck mute. At any other time, she might have laughed at their comical expressions.

"Why are you here, Mitch? Has something happened?" She remembered asking him to check on her parents. "Oh, no." A wave of dizziness assailed her. "My parents…"

"They're fine," Mitch assured before she could finish. Concerned, he moved toward her, then stopped, sandy-blond brows raised when he saw Antonio put a supportive, *possessive* arm across her shoulders.

Antonio extended his free hand. "We have spoken on the telephone. I am Antonio Castillo, and may I assume you are Chelsa's detective from Vicksburg?"

"Not hers exclusively," Mitch said with a boyish grin that would surely cause women's hearts to flutter. "But close enough. Glad to meet you. I'm right pleased y'all have moved to the palace." His deep, Southern accent gave him a friendly, approachable air, but undercurrents of steel were evident in his sharp blue eyes.

"We thought it was for the best."

Chelsa glanced from Mitch to Cole and Joseph. She had an idea all this "getting to know you" stuff was a stalling tactic. And Cole Martinez appeared to be holding something behind his back. To a man, they looked like a bunch of cats with the cream still on their whiskers. "What is it you all don't want to tell me?"

Cole heaved a sigh and exchanged a look with Joseph. Both men knew and respected the stubbornness of women. Their wives had taught them well. "She has a right to know," he said for Mitch's benefit, then stepped forward and handed her a slip of paper. "Try not to touch it too much."

They intended to dust it for prints, she surmised. A weight of dread settled in her stomach. There would be no need as far as she was concerned.

She recognized the stationery.

Rick's.

It said something about his state of mind, his brazenness, that he'd send a missive that blatantly shouted his identity.

Gingerly holding the buff-colored paper by the edges, she glanced down at the familiar handwriting. Her hands trembled and the words blurred.

Antonio steadied her, held her and read over her shoulder.

The warning was short and to the point, and Chelsa felt as though she were holding a venomous snake in her hands.

"You will have found the quarter and know its meaning. Don't think you can hide behind your classy prince. It will be a sad day for the sports world, but I promise you, I'll cut him down to get to you. You can't run, and you can't hide. Watch for me, darling."

Even though Tony's warmth was at her back, she shivered, feeling chilled to the bone, trapped in the icy fingers of shock.

My God, they'd been making love out in the open—she'd been putting Antonio Castillo at risk.

Dimly she heard Antonio swear, felt his arms tightened around her. As much as she wanted to lean into him, to beseech him to make it all go away, to make it better, she couldn't.

None of her rationalizations would work anymore.

Fairy tales were her business, but she'd never let herself dream for the realization of one.

Until just recently.

With Tony.

The sinister words on the paper before her blurred

into an inky blob as her heart sank like a cement weight in her chest.

With her head in the clouds she'd let down her guard, allowed herself to dream, allowed herself to want it all.

The fairy tale.

The prince.

Oh, not the castle and title and all the royal hoopla that went with it, but the love, the utter single-minded devotion she sensed deep in her heart that Antonio could give.

But if she reached for the dream, she would relegate his life to the status of hers. He, too, would forever be looking over his shoulder because of Rick. Rick would use Antonio to hunt her, use his popularity of being revered in the limelight.

Just as he would use Emily and Sophie if she gave him the chance.

She could control the surroundings of her children, try to keep them safe, even if it meant running for the rest of their lives.

But she couldn't control Antonio—or the royal family—from conducting their lives in the open...

In plain sight of a mad man.

Coming to a decision, the only choice she could make, she stepped out of his comforting hold and carefully handed the paper back to Cole.

"The girls and I will leave right away."

"No," Antonio said, turning her to face him. "You will not. This letter is nothing but a scare tactic. You are still safest here."

Safest. That single word left a wide margin of doubt. "Rick is unstable, Tony, and he means what he says. We can have fingerprint tests run till the cows come home, but I know his handwriting. He wrote that warning and he managed to get it here—'' She glanced at Detective D'Ambra. ''I assume it was delivered here?'' There was always the possibility that Mitch brought it with him.

Mitch nodded. ''Cole and Joseph showed it to me when I arrived.''

''And why did you, by the way?'' she asked. ''Arrive, that is.''

He shrugged. ''A hunch. I got frustrated when Vicksburg lost your ex-husband's trail. I had some vacation time wastin' away and figured I'd come on over and check on you, spend a little time with Martinez.''

Come on over, as in cross an ocean, Chelsa thought. What the slow-walking, slow-talking detective didn't say, but what was very evident, was that he'd been worried.

And he had every right to be. Now, more than ever, Chelsa had to convince Tony, the daredevil who had no fear, that there was indeed something to fear.

If not for himself, then for his family.

She reached out and touched the front of Antonio's shirt, her eyes pleading for understanding, her brain memorizing every detail of his handsome face. He had a hero's heart, and he would stick by his vow to protect her.

But the stakes were too high.

She drew in a trembling breath, gathering every bit of emotional strength she possessed. The time had come to step away, and it was the hardest thing she'd ever had to do in her life.

Because she loved him she had to let him go.

''If Rick can get a sick warning note through the

guards, he can find a way to get to you or your family. I don't want to be responsible for that." Her mind made up, she glanced at Cole. Fear was like a living entity within her, but she tried to ignore it, tried to be strong.

"Cole, could I impose on you to find me a discreet way out of Valldoria? The girls and I can be packed and ready in about twenty minutes."

She noticed that Cole glanced at Antonio, as though seeking permission. That upset her. Darn it, every man in the room was looking at him as though he were king. Had they all forgotten he only claimed to be the spare?

With a frustrated sigh, she turned toward the door. Antonio's soft words stopped her in midstep.

"If you insist on leaving, I will follow."

She swallowed back wimpy tears and whirled around, her nerves stretched past the breaking point. Didn't he know what this was doing to her? "Don't be an idiot!"

Three sets of male brows shot up at her calling the spare prince an idiot. Well, so what. If he wouldn't have a care for his own safety, somebody had to run the show.

Prince Joseph laughed, breaking some of the tension in the room. "Please, Chelsa, do us the honor of staying. Not many can render my brother speechless and I, for one, am quite enjoying the entertainment."

She figured it would be stretching the bounds of protocol to tell a crown prince where to go.

Antonio, apparently, had no such problem. He said something rude and terse to Joseph, never taking his eyes off Chelsa, pinning her to the spot with the force of his gaze.

"My promise still stands. If you leave, I will follow."

"Your threat, you mean?"

"Take it as you will."

Like two predators faced off in battle, neither one willing to give up territory, they stared at each other.

Chelsa was the first to back down. She huffed out a sigh, feeling boxed in, feeling relieved and scared and so mixed-up, she couldn't lock on to a single emotion for more than a fleeting second. "I'm trying to protect you, Tony. And your family."

"I have told you before, *querida,* I can take care of myself. Cole will see to the family." He stepped closer, took unfair advantage with both his words and his touch. "Think of your children, Chelsa. Stay."

"Don't pull that on me again." The demand was a weak one. Why couldn't she be stronger? It was awful to deliberately, continually, drag these people into her private hell.

"Stay," he said again, softly.

She closed her eyes. "This is my fight."

"Stay."

"Stop saying that."

"I will, when you agree." His palms cupped her cheeks, his thumb lifting her chin.

She met the determination in his brown eyes, knew she was no match for it.

Knew that he was right. As much as she was loath to put them all in danger, the prospect of harm befalling her children was too horrible to bear. At least here they had a better chance.

The only thing she could do was agree.

But in agreeing, she would have to avoid Antonio, isolate herself.

If Rick found a way in and came gunning for her, she had to make sure no one else was in the line of fire.

And creating that distance would serve two purposes. It would prepare her for when she and Antonio truly had to part, would make it easier.

And she could tell herself that all she wanted, when she knew darned well it was a lie.

It would never be easy to part from Antonio.

Chapter Fourteen

Chelsa was definitely avoiding him, which left Antonio in a constant state of frustration. He couldn't remember the last time he'd spent so much time with his family—although he was a little surprised by how much he enjoyed it.

A week had passed with no threat or sign of Rick Lawrence. Regardless, it was ridiculous for her to avoid him—particularly since he knew she was doing it out of some misguided attempt to protect *him*.

¡Dios! Did the woman not understand about a man's pride? He would have to remind her of the water baby story of masculinity. Well, perhaps that one wasn't the exact example he was looking for, but it was close. And damn it, he wanted Chelsa close.

His heart actually stumbled when he looked up and saw her coming out of the solarium—the room she'd been using to do her writing. He'd even wandered in there a time or two and checked her work in progress.

It seemed Valldoria was good for her—her stories were coming alive. The latest segment had already been delivered to the post office by one of the palace guards.

But All Work And No Play was a motto that made

him itch under the collar. And by the looks of the shadows beneath Chelsa's eyes, it was wearing her down.

The sight of that weariness made his heart turn over in his chest. He wanted this ordeal over with, wanted Chelsa by his side, carefree, happy. She deserved an easier time.

He stepped into her path. "Rescue me, *bella*."

He saw the way her blue eyes flared with excitement, saw the mask come down, saw her hesitate.

"Ah, you are caught and you might as well be good about it. You have been working like a demon and I am feeling quite the bum." He held out his hand. "Come. Take a walk with me in the sunshine. Let me listen to that sweet Southern voice."

Her lips turned up in a reluctant smile. "You're so full of it, Prince."

He tsked. "Now, now. Do not be elevating my status. Especially within hearing of my brother. He will put me to work."

"I've seen you working this week, and it didn't look as though anybody was twisting your arm. You're a fraud, Antonio Castillo."

"Ah, you do know how to put my ego in its place. Although I am happy to hear you admit you have watched me—especially since you have been so adept at avoiding me."

Chelsa laughed. Oh, she had missed him. "I don't think there's a place big enough to hold your ego." She didn't acknowledge or deny his comment about avoidance. "But regardless, you're far from a bum."

The sound of chisels meeting stone echoed from the high ceilings. She looked up. A balcony where minstrels serenaded on special occasions was covered with plastic as masons busily worked on some sort of statue. It was this noise that had distracted her from working and had caused her to run into Antonio, something she *had* been avoiding lately.

Now her curiosity got the better of her.

"What are they doing up there?"

"Carving statues of Joseph and Briana."

"Why?"

"It is a tradition. The likeness of all kings and princes are rendered when they marry. Briana insisted she would not be chiseled though, while pregnant, and the masons have waited. Now, however, she is butting heads with them artistically over Joseph's statue. She is determined they get his expression just right." He lowered his voice and glanced around as though he were about to impart something forbidden. "The masons are adamantly refusing to sculpt their crown prince laughing like a hyena."

She loved the way he added drama to his storytelling, could spend a lifetime just listening to that sexy Latin accent. "I'm sure that's not what she meant."

Antonio laughed. "You are right. Though tradition has always dictated a reserved, staid rendering, Briana feels Joseph's should reflect his new persona."

"You mean he didn't used to grin like a besotted fool?"

"Do not let him hear you say that."

"I think it'll make a nice change. He and his princess are so obviously in love. It's hard to imagine that Raquel's statue might have been the one standing next to his."

"Now *there* would have been a stoic replica if ever there was one."

"I adore Briana, but I can't imagine anyone not being crazy over Raquel."

"That is love, I suppose. It strikes where least expected." His voice went incredibly soft and the look he gave her made her mouth go dry. It was as though he were speaking of himself. Good night, she must be more tired than she thought. It was just those sort of fantasies that played cruel games with her heart.

"I imagine Cole's thankful there were no feelings between Joseph and Raquel."

"Thankful is much too tame. Cole and Rocky are perfect for each other." He held out his elbow. "So, madam, would you care to take a turn around the gardens with me? I, for one, am quite ready to escape this noise."

Chelsa hesitated, then finally placed her hand in the crook of his elbow. She *was* going a little stir-crazy. And when she got this close to Antonio, she was weak.

Before they made it to the front door, Emily and Sophie came streaking around the corner, wearing matching, bright pink bathing suits.

"Momma!" Sophie yelled above the racket of the mason's chisels. "I swimmed wif'out the floaties!"

"You didn't swim," Emily debated. "You just doggie-paddled."

"So? Irish doggie-paddled, too."

Chelsa looked at Antonio. "The dog went swimming?" she asked faintly. Then she looked back at the girls. "Next time I'll come watch." She felt guilty over leaving her daughters in the care of Antonio's family so much lately.

Subconsciously she'd been avoiding everyone—including her own children. Rick's beef was with her.

If he found her before the authorities got to him, she didn't want anyone else nearby.

Her heart swelled with overwhelming love as she gazed at her daughters. She'd made Antonio promise to care for them if something happened to her. She knew he'd uphold that vow, make sure the kids got to her parents. And his family would be right there to lend an emotional hand. They were good people.

But, oh, the thought of being parted from her children was intolerable, wrenched her heart.

"Did you get your work done?" Emily asked, forgetting about arguing with her sister.

"Yes." Chelsa couldn't resist touching Emily's baby-soft hair, stroking Sophie's pudgy cheek. "Antonio and I were just about to go out for some fresh air."

"Can we come?"

She hesitated, saw the disappointment in her daughters' eyes and gave in. The grounds were well protected. Photos of Rick had been distributed all over town and security was on twenty-four-hour alert. They were safe. And she had to be careful not to thrust her own fears onto her daughters. "Sure."

"Wait for me," Briana said, appearing in the hallway with baby Joseph in her arms. "I've had it with those pigheaded masons and their racket. Every time I try to communicate, they look at me like I'm speaking a different language!"

Chelsa started to point out that maybe there *was* a language barrier. Briana was obviously American.

Then Joseph came up behind his wife. "I must remind the workmen how fluent you are in languages, *querida*. I would not want them to speak ill about you, unaware that you can understand."

"Speak ill?" she said, her voice raising above the din. "All I said was that they had the lips wrong. You have wonderful lips, Joseph, and the workmen were getting entirely too chisel-happy in that area."

Joseph smiled and kissed his wife. "Let us move out-of-doors. If we escape the noise for a bit, it will likely improve all of our dispositions."

"Amen to that," Queen Isabel said, looking thoroughly composed even as she chased the wet puppy through the hall. A bedraggled cat followed at a more dignified pace, stopping every now and again to shake a damp paw.

Chelsa's eyes widened and she looked at her daughters. "You took Señor Gatito swimming, too?"

"Yep," Sophie announced. "But he didn't like it. And I told Emily, but she didn't listen."

Emily gathered steam to level a comeback, but the queen intervened before Chelsa could.

"Everyone must try something they do not like at least once. Otherwise they will never know what they are missing." She was looking at Antonio as she said the words, which seemed to have a deeper meaning.

A meaning that everyone in the room apparently understood except Chelsa.

Antonio got his mother's meaning, and it slammed into him with the force of a raging bull. He thought about the story he'd read—Chelsa's latest.

A story about a black sheep among fleecy white ones, whose fur was washed and curled and bedecked with bows. With long, flirty eyelashes, the fluffy sheep pranced around with brightly painted toenails that matched their bows. The black sheep, on the other hand, had hair flopping in his eyes and dirt on his hooves and a grin so wide, everybody just had to love him. He was always pulling outrageous stunts for attention and wallowing in the dirt and having fun.

Then one day, a huge, pouring rain came down and drenched Andy, the black sheep, which he thought was great fun, until he noticed that the downpour had swept a wandering baby sheep into the pond. Since Andy considered himself somewhat of a hero, he immediately jumped into the water to save the fleecy white baby. When he came out, he was astonished to find that his own furry coat was white and fluffy. For the first time in his life, he realized he could blend in, that he didn't need to show off and scare everybody to death with his antics.

And while Andy the sheep pondered this new turn of events, resisting it even, the Sophie water baby hopped onto his back and told him he had always been part of the family. But they all knew and respected the fact that he didn't want bows and ribbons like everybody else, so the mama sheep concentrated on keeping the other sheep groomed. But that didn't mean the mama sheep or brother and sister sheep loved him any less. He was always part of their flock, no matter what his color.

Because family was about love.

Antonio felt his lips pull upward as he remembered the cute story. Putting his arm around Chelsa, he looked at the queen and grinned, knowing that in her silent way, his mother was telling him that relationships and commitment weren't such a bad thing.

A fact that he'd already figured out all on his own.

But now wasn't the time to announce that fact. Chelsa's story had just put one of the missing pieces in place for him.

Subconsciously he'd been searching for completion, and incredibly, he'd sought that in thrill seeking. But it wasn't enough. He knew that now. Just like duty hadn't been enough for Joseph. His brother had gone out searching for love, and evidently the saints had been listening because he'd been led to Briana.

Had Antonio, in turn, been led in much the same way through the freak boating accident to Chelsa's doorstep? And her heart?

That slippery moss under his feet had already started to wear away. Knowing Chelsa, making love with her, had turned everything he believed about himself upside down. She made him rethink his life-long aversion to commitment. In the past week—while Chelsa had been doing her best to avoid him—he'd had plenty of time on his hands to notice the happy couples around him, the changes in both Joseph and Raquel, the glow that was still present between his parents even after thirty-five years of marriage.

Just like the little black sheep in Chelsa's water baby story, he realized he'd been so busy running from nonexistent shadows, that he'd missed what was truly important. Family. Love. He realized that all his running had really been an elaborate search.

A search for the one person who was the perfect complement to himself.

His soul mate.

Chelsa.

But she had a stubborn streak a mile wide. It might take some doing to get past that, but he felt he was up to the task.

He looked down at her, wishing they were alone. "Let's get out of here before we have the whole city on our walk," Antonio said.

"There are plenty of grounds, my son," Isabel admonished. "If you wish for privacy, we will certainly afford it to you. Come, *niñas,*" she said to the girls. "Let us corral these animals and encourage them to dry off in the sunshine. Cole and Raquel have just arrived around back. They were delayed by that wonderfully Southern detective, but they will be along any minute now. And I noticed that Raquel has brought camera equipment. I believe she intends to use the water gardens as her latest backdrop." Holding each of the girls by a hand, she ushered them to the front door. "How do you feel about frog costumes, hmm? I believe Señora Raquel intends to do a water baby exposé as a tribute to your mother."

The girls chorused their enthusiasm for the subject matter, and Chelsa let Antonio lead her out the door.

"Never in my wildest dreams would I have imagined the royal family hanging around outside." Chelsa remarked. The palace was like a small city. If everyone wanted to escape the noise, there were plenty of extra wings to choose from that would insulate them well enough.

"Actually, we are like everyday people."

She raised a brow at that.

"Seriously," he said. "Wait until the fiesta this coming weekend, and you will see. My family goes all out, and joins in."

"There's a fiesta this weekend?" Her heart lurched. This past week without incident had lulled her into a false sense of security.

"Yes. Provided the masons finish their project."

"You're going to celebrate the statues of the prince and princess?" Distracted, she glanced around at the beautiful gardens, trying to shake the niggling sense of impending doom, hating that she'd turned into such a worrier, that her life had been reduced to this.

"Of course. We have fiestas and blessings of everything from hedgehogs to our grand *toros*. A likeness of our crown prince and his bride are cause for celebration. Have you not noticed the delivery trucks in and out of the gates of late?"

Yes, she had, and it made her nervous. But she was a guest here and couldn't very well ask them to change their plans and traditions on her account. She'd been enough of a disruption as it was. "What are you going to do? Conduct tours of the palace or move the stone figures outside?"

"We will—" His words halted as a popping noise sounded simultaneously with the bark of an oak tree exploding.

"*¡Dios!* Get down!" Antonio reacted instinctively, dragging Chelsa to the ground and covering her with his body. His heart thundered in his chest and adrenaline shot through him as he reached down and snatched a .38 from his boot.

Chelsa, looking dazed, stared at the gun in his hand, but he didn't have time to stop and explain that he'd been packing a piece since they'd returned to Valldoria.

"What...?"

"That was a bullet. Someone's shooting at us." A ridiculously generic statement, he realized. He knew who that someone was.

He scanned the area, saw a flash of white. A uniform. A delivery uniform.

His jaw clenched and his hand tightened around the gun. He couldn't make out features from this distance, but he knew with a certainty deep in his bones that

Rick Lawrence had somehow managed to breach security, had slipped past the gates, masquerading as a delivery person.

Slipped past with the sole intention of exacting revenge on Chelsa.

At a palace surrounded by half the Royal Guard. *A fool,* Antonio thought. The man had obviously gone mad. And that unstableness of mind made the situation all the more dangerous.

And deadly.

At the moment, no one was paying attention to the fact that he and Chelsa were huddled on the ground. Obviously, Lawrence was using a silencer. The roaring splash of the fountain would have prevented the occupants of the courtyard from hearing the thump of the bullet.

"What are we going to do?" Chelsa asked, voice trembling, chest heaving.

"Shh." He shifted, pinpointing Cole's position, trying to get his friend's attention. Cole was a suspicious man by nature, and thankfully, now was no exception. He saw Cole's shoulders go rigid, saw understanding dawn, saw Martinez and the Mississippi detective draw their weapons.

He also saw Emily and Sophie.

They'd wandered away from his mother to trail their fingers in the splashing fountain.

And they were wide open—without even a bush to shield them from the force of a bullet.

Everything within him went absolutely, rigidly still. He lived his life facing challenges head-on, never gave it a second thought, enjoyed it even, the thrill of conquering new heights.

¡Madre de Dios! This was no thrill-seeking danger situation. It was for real.

Life-shatteringly important.

Chelsa and her little girls had become his world.

But the babies were too far away. If he went to them, Chelsa would be left unprotected.

Indecision pumped through Antonio.

With her heart trying to beat its way out of her chest, Chelsa raised up, searched the distance…and looked straight into the eyes of evil.

He wore a cap, and had a mustache—a disguise. But she recognized him. Recognized that build, that cocky stance.

"Oh, God, it's Rick!" She fought the scream that lodged in her throat. She knew Rick's single-minded determination, knew he wasn't bluffing when he stepped out from behind the oak and blatantly pointed a gun.

Directly at them.

"My kids!" She saw them by the fountain, felt nausea and dizziness swamp her. With a strength born of a mother's terror, she ripped from Antonio's arms and took off across the expanse of lawn toward her children.

Antonio was less than a pace behind. A round of bullets whizzed past as they sprinted toward the courtyard. "Stay down, damn it!"

Her lungs burned and her eyes stung. "Please, God!" she prayed.

Antonio snatched her hand, nearly pulling her off balance, shielding her. She tried to tug away, wanting both hands free, wanting her arms filled with her babies, wanting Antonio far enough away from her so he wasn't in the line of fire.

The commotion and their urgency brought the Royal Guard, *and* the royal family running.

One of Chelsa's worst nightmares.

Emily and Sophie, alerted to the danger, stood like frightened rabbits trapped in the path of a cobra.

Joseph was forcibly restraining the queen from going after the girls, jockeying for position to run the race himself.

Didn't these people have a care for their safety? Their duty? If one of them was maimed or killed, it would be her fault. She'd brought this down on their heads.

All because the man she'd married and thought she'd loved had turned out to be a stranger. A madman.

But right now her children were her first priority.

Cole, with his gun drawn was shouting orders and the Royal Guard was fanning out, creating a human barrier between the direction of the bullets and Chelsa's children, as well as the royal family.

Chelsa wanted to scream, but her voice wouldn't work. She felt like her legs were lead weights, carrying her in slow motion.

The girls started to run toward them.

"No!" Chelsa screamed. "Stay there! Get down!"

The sound of Chelsa's terror ripped Antonio apart. He never gave a thought to the danger—at least in the sense of it having a pull of intrigue that beaconed him to conquer. He was fueled by anger and love, the unholy terror of harm befalling Chelsa and his girls.

And he was scared spitless.

Trying to determine the direction of the bullets, trying to use his own body to shield Chelsa even as she resisted him, he reached the girls first, hooked an arm around each and kept on running.

He thrust Emily into Raquel's arms, and Chelsa, along with Sophie, into the queen's hold, then whirled around, intent on shoving that silencer down Rick Lawrence's throat.

"Antonio, no!" Chelsa yelled, grabbing at him even as she struggled to fill her arms with her daughters.

He spared a bare instant to look back at her, to drink in the sight of the three of them, mother and daughters, his heart's desire.

The words *I love you* backed up in his throat. There would be time later for declarations. He hoped. Right now, though, he would see an end to her torment. He would make sure Lawrence was out of her life, once and for all.

Out of *their* lives.

"Stay put."

Joseph and Cole fell into step beside him, as did Detective D'Ambra. Antonio frowned, the stock of the gun slick in his hands. "Joseph, this is my fight. Stay with your family. You, too, Cole."

Cole ignored him. Commanding the Royal Guard was his job.

Joseph, wearing an equally lethal expression as he palmed a gun Cole had given him, shook his head. "We are in this together, brother. This is about family."

"Then stay the hell out of my way. I want first crack at the scum."

No one argued. The look on Antonio's face prevented it.

He noticed that Lawrence was hesitating now, his

fevered gaze darting around at the army of guards closing in.

Antonio's steps became measured now. Calm descended. He could take him out, get this over with. He raised his arm, pointing the .38.

Someone shouted and a guard stepped in front of him, then another, blowing his shot. Gunfire erupted as Cole's men rushed Lawrence.

In the scuffle, one man went down. One of Cole's men.

It took five more to wrestle Rick to the ground, to disarm him.

Deadly calm, Antonio waded through the authorities. His gun was steady in his outstretched arm, and pointed straight at Rick Lawrence's heart.

"It's over, Tony," Joseph said, placing a restraining hand on his arm.

Antonio stared down at the man who'd made Chelsa's life so miserable, feeling both pity and hatred. He wanted to tear this piece of scum apart with his bare hands. But that wasn't necessary.

Just a little squeeze of the trigger would do it.

His finger tightened.

"It's not worth it, *mi hermano,*" Joseph said quietly.

Was it? Antonio wondered. It felt like it at the moment. He thought of Chelsa's softness and sweet spirit, of little Sophie's wide-eyed innocence and rambling stories, and of Emily's infectious giggle and penchant for flattery. Rick Lawrence threw away that great family and Antonio was fortunate enough to get them. Joseph was right. There was no need to come to them with blood on his hands.

He eased his finger off the trigger, dropped his

hand to his side and looked at his brother. "I trust you'll do your prince thing and make sure the charges against this guy are so airtight that the threat of parole will never again be an issue?"

"Between Father and myself, I am certain we can manage that." The strict laws in Valldoria were the prime reason Chelsa had been sent to his country in the first place.

"Good. Now I've got a family to see to. You wanted a ringside seat to watch my fall, brother. I am offering you front-row tickets."

Leaving the Royal Guard to take Rick Lawrence into custody, Antonio dropped his gun back into his boot and turned toward the palace.

Toward his destiny.

For a guy who spent his life more or less determined to be a loner, the commitment of family by his side had the profound effect of locking that final piece of the puzzle firmly in place.

Family is what living was all about. And love.

He would get both with Chelsa.

Elation started deep in his belly and worked its way upward. The closer he got to them, the wider his grin grew. He felt cocky and on top of the world now that the adrenaline was subsiding. He felt like a conquistador returning victoriously to claim his bride.

But the look on Chelsa's face told him she was anything but impressed.

"You idiot! What in the world possessed you to charge off like that? It's just like you…a—a *playboy* who's so caught up in your pursuit of thrill seeking that you don't give a single thought to the people around you who happen to love you!"

Amused by her outburst, he pounced on her last

statement. "Ah, *querida,* may I assume you are including yourself in the list of those who love me?"

Chelsa was certain she could hit him right now. She'd never been so scared in her life. How dare he go off, deliberately put himself in danger. And then make a stupid joke when she tried to tell him how special he was!

Flustered, she didn't bother to censor her words. "It would serve you right if I did, Mr. Run-From-Commitment-Castillo!"

"Prince Antonio, if you please," he corrected.

Antonio *never* acknowledged his title, and the fact that he did so now, caused the royal family to stare at him in varying degrees of surprise—all except Queen Isabel, who looked smug.

But Chelsa was the most astonished of all. Butterflies took wing in her stomach. Could it be? Antonio had always equated title with commitment and sworn he didn't want any part of either. But...

"You did not answer, *querida.* Are you among those who love me?"

Well, of course she was, but she wasn't about to tip her hand so easily. It would do this playboy prince good to worry.

The charismatic twinkle in his eyes waned, replaced by such profound tenderness, everyone present forgot to take a breath—including Chelsa.

"I love you, Chelsa Lawrence. I never thought I'd say this, but I've got marriage in mind. Will you be my princess? Live with me in my castle? Love me?"

At that moment, she couldn't have spoken if her life depended on it. Antonio mistook her vocal paralysis for indecision and set about to persuade her. He cupped her face and kissed her so softly, so reverently, her heart nearly flopped out of her chest.

She didn't know if she could draw sufficient breath to speak. "My ex-husband's a felon."

He drew back, looked at her with so much love, it nearly blinded. "Do you think that matters to me? I don't care who you are, or where you're from, or anything else about your past—as long as you say you love me, as long as you'll promise to share my life."

"Oh, Tony…I don't need the castle and all the trappings," she whispered.

He smiled. "That's one of the things I love about you. You have so much integrity, so much strength. From the moment we met, I have watched you in awe. You don't run or back down from tight spots. You humble me, *querida*. You will also keep me grounded."

She would give him the attention he'd always sought—not because of who he was or could be. Just for him, the man.

Her arms rose, her fingers linking behind his neck. He saw her surrender, her love.

His heart pounded. Until this moment, he hadn't realized how scared he was. Scared that she wouldn't return his love.

That smile he loved so much blossomed on her face. A face he intended to spend a lifetime looking at, one that he would never tire of.

"Come to think of it, you could use somebody to keep you grounded."

"I'm sinking, *bella*. Just three small words will save my life."

She touched the deep crease in his cheek, eased right up against him, feeling safe, home at last.

Home in his arms.

"The words aren't small, Tony. They're bigger than anything I ever imagined I could feel. I love you. And if you've really got marriage in mind, I accept."

He lifted her off the ground, whirled her around and kissed her with an expertise that made her knees weak—an expertise he should *not* have displayed in public.

But Chelsa wasn't complaining. She was right where she wanted to be.

"Mother," Antonio said. "You will get your wish after all. Both your sons married by age thirty—as per tradition."

Chelsa thought to object. "I'm not sure I like being labeled a tradition."

"Ah, the very best tradition, my love." He reached out and brought Emily and Sophie into their circle. His family. "Let me introduce you all to the newest princess of Valldoria. And you, *mi bellas,*" he said to the girls, "will be princesses also."

"Nuh-uh," Sophie declared, frowning. "*I'm* the mermaid!"

"Hush, silly," Emily scolded, even though her mother and Antonio were too busy kissing to notice Sophie's outburst. "A princess is better than a mermaid."

Sophie wasn't too sure of that. Sometimes Emily said stuff just so she could be better and smarter cuz she was older. As long as Antonio could be her daddy, though, she guessed it might be all right to be a princess.

So she folded her pudgy hands together and turned round eyes up to her momma and her new daddy, her little mind already spinning stories.

Maybe the frog in the water babies stories was a prince who looked like Antonio. Yep, she bet he was, that sneaky thing. She should'a seed it before, with his big old sad eyes just waiting for the right baby to set him free.

And she'd make sure it was the Sophie baby who got to kiss the frog, *not* the Emily baby.

Well…maybe that wasn't so nice.

Maybe there could be *two* frogs.…

*This holiday season, dash to
the delivery room with*

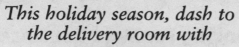

The McIntyre brothers of Bison City, Wyoming,
have no idea they're about to become daddies—
until a little stork tells them to hustle down to
the delivery room!

*Don't miss this exciting new series from three of
your favorite American Romance® authors!*

**October 1999
BABY BY MIDNIGHT?**
by Karen Toller Whittenburg (#794)

**November 1999
COUNTDOWN TO BABY**
by Muriel Jensen (#798)

**December 1999
BABY 2000**
by Judy Christenberry (#802)

Available wherever Harlequin books are sold.

LOOK OUT FOR SOME FAST AND LOOSE MATCHMAKING FROM

HARLEQUIN®

A M E R I C A N ◆ R O M A N C E®

Cathy Gillen Thacker once again brings her special brand of down-home romance to a *new* four-book miniseries

The McCabes of Texas

John and Lilah McCabe have four of the sexiest sons Laramie, Texas, has ever seen—but no grandbabies! Now they're fixin' to get a whole passel of 'em.

September 1999—#789 **DR. COWBOY**
Cathy's 50th Harlequin book!

October 1999—#793 **WILDCAT COWBOY**

November 1999—#797 **A COWBOY'S WOMAN**

December 1999—#801 **A COWBOY KIND OF DADDY**

Round 'em up at a store near you!

HARLEQUIN®
Makes any time special ™

3 Stories of Holiday Romance from three bestselling Harlequin® authors

Valentine Babies

by

ANNE STUART

TARA TAYLOR QUINN

JULE McBRIDE

Goddess in Waiting by Anne Stuart
Edward walks into Marika's funky maternity shop to pick up some things for his sister. He doesn't expect to assist in the delivery of a baby and fall for outrageous Marika.

Gabe's Special Delivery by Tara Taylor Quinn
On February 14, Gabe Stone finds a living, breathing valentine on his doorstep—his daughter. Her mother has given Gabe four hours to adjust to fatherhood, resolve custody and win back his ex-wife?

My Man Valentine by Jule McBride
Everyone knows Eloise Hunter and C. D. Valentine are in love. Except Eloise and C. D. Then, one of Eloise's baby-sitting clients leaves her with a baby to mind, and C. D. swings into protector mode.

VALENTINE BABIES

On sale January 2000 at your favorite retail outlet.

HARLEQUIN®
Makes any time special ™

Visit us at www.romance.net   PHVALB

HARLEQUIN®
AMERICAN ◆ ROMANCE®

Wishes you a very
Merry Christmas!

From our home to yours…this Christmas,
Harlequin American Romance® brings
you two special romances to light up
the holiday season!

In December 1999 don't miss:

SAVING CHRISTMAS (#803)
by **Pamela Bauer**
The little town of Christmas is in trouble—
can Sara Richards warm the heart of sexy
Joe "Scrooge" Gibson in time to save it?

MISTLETOE DADDY (#804)
by **Jacqueline Diamond**
Marnie Afton is stunned when Tom Jakes
comes back to town with his little son! Will she
finally receive the best gift of all this Christmas?

Warm your heart with Harlequin American Romance®!

Available at your favorite retail outlet.

◆ HARLEQUIN®
Makes any time special ™

Visit us at: www.romance.net

HARCHRIS